charm

&

strange

charm
&
strange

stephanie kuehn

 st. martin's griffin ≈ new york

CHARM & STRANGE. Copyright © 2013 by Stephanie Kuehn. All rights reserved. Printed in the United States of America. For information, address St. Martin's Press, 175 Fifth Avenue, New York, N.Y. 10010.

www.stmartins.com

Designed by Anna Gorovoy

The Library of Congress has cataloged the hardcover edition as follows:

Kuehn, Stephanie.
    Charm & strange / Stephanie Kuehn.—First edition.
        p. cm.
    ISBN 978-1-250-02194-6 (hardcover)
    ISBN 978-1-250-02193-9 (e-book)
1. Psychological abuse—Ficton.   2. Mental illness—Fiction.   3. Sexual abuse—Fiction.   I. Title.   II. Title: Charm and strange.
    PZ7.K94872Ch 2013
    [Fic]—dc23

                                                    2013003247

ISBN 978-1-250-04917-9 (trade paperback)

St. Martin's Griffin books may be purchased for educational, business, or promotional use. For information on bulk purchases, please contact Macmillan Corporate and Premium Sales Department at 1-800-221-7945, extension 5442, or write specialmarkets@macmillan.com.

First St. Martin's Griffin Trade Paperback Edition: June 2014

10 9 8 7 6 5 4 3 2 1

for will. for everything.

before

chapter

one

matter

I don't feel the presence of God here.

I pace along the far side of the river, my ears filled with the hum of cicadas and the roar of water flowing over the milldam. Vermont is postcard perfect. I could stand on my toes and peer over the current and the cattails and see the whole town spread before me. Green-shuttered houses. The cobblestone square. The church spire. The boarding school.

But I don't.

I crave the illusion of solitude.

The dark-haired girl, who looks like a boy, watches me from the woods. She's hunkered down in a birch thicket with bare legs and discerning eyes. I know what she saw and I don't want her to talk to me, but she'll try. I'm sure of this. She mistakes my distance for mystery, and she wants to know why I do the things I do.

My sister was the same way. She thought there was a reason for everything.

Me? I don't think there's a reason for anything.

Not anymore.

Seven years ago, I strode onto the local country club court beneath a punishing Charlottesville sun like a mini Roger Federer. I had the headband. The tennis whites. The killer instinct.

I was nine.

My opponent was Soren Nichols, a nobody compared to me, top seed in the U10 bracket. But I was off my game, got in trouble early. Soren, who had a decent serve and quick feet, easily took advantage of my unforced errors and double faults.

It didn't take long. I didn't know how to come from behind. I lost in straight sets in front of the home crowd. Without so much as a glance in the direction of my parents or my coach, I stalked to the net and reached across to shake Soren's hand.

"Good game," I said through clenched teeth.

"Thanks, Drew. You too." He had a sheepish grin and southern drawl.

Something dark roiled in my gut. A subterranean shift.

No, that was not a good game. Not for me.

People got to their feet between matches, milling across the court, the club grounds. I trailed Soren as his mother hugged him and his father clapped his back. Then I slipped into the narrow alley that ran back toward the clubhouse and waited in the shadows beneath the grandstand.

When he passed by, I stepped onto the walkway. No one could see us.

"Hey," I said softly.

Soren turned. I took my racket, reached behind me, and cracked it full force across the side of his face. Then I jumped back and gave a little yell of surprise. Like I didn't know what had happened.

That's exactly what I told everyone when I ran for help. *I don't know. I don't know, I don't know how he got hurt. I was running. Maybe I slipped. Maybe he fell. I don't* know.

I shook with shame, not regret. Soren was out cold. When he first came to, he really didn't know. All that swelling. The blood.

An ambulance came. Then a cop car.

When pressed harder about it, I cried. A lot.

Howled, really.

"Why'd you let them do that?" the girl asks as she crawls from the bushes. She holds the headphones of her mp3 player carefully in one hand. Her hair's so short, it's practically a Caesar cut, but she still has to brush dirt and leaves out of it now that she's standing in the open.

I edge away from her. Play dumb. Yeah, I know she's a transfer student, and sure, we have a class together and she just joined the cross-country team, but it's not like any of that means I want to have an actual conversation with her. Why would I? No one around here ever talks to me without reason.

None of them good.

"Do what?" I ask cautiously.

"Let them get away with pushing you while you were . . . you know." She points to my leg. It's soaked with piss—my own, courtesy of two classmates who decided to assault me on their way back to campus. And no, I didn't fight back. I never do. That wouldn't be fair.

Besides, there's not a lot you can do when somebody punches you midstream.

The girl clears her throat. She's waiting for my answer, but I step up my playing-dumb game by saying nothing.

She frowns. "So you're just cool with being treated like that?"

Like what? I wonder, but give a careless shrug. "Kind of looks that way."

There's silence and squinting. Her ears aren't even pierced and she's wearing oversized athletic shorts that look cheap, like something you'd find in the clearance aisle at CVS. They drape past her knees and bear the silver-and-black logo of some professional sports team. Her whole look is at odds with the rest of the girls around here, who like to show off as much skin as possible, every inch of them tanned, coltish, and prep school sleek. This girl is different. This girl is forgettable.

She speaks again. "You really okay?"

"Why wouldn't I be?"

"It's just, you seem, I don't know, sort of strange."

I nod and run a hand through my hair. I'm not wondering anything anymore. I don't want to know what she's thinking.

"I'm fine," I mutter.

"So where're you from? I don't recognize your accent."

My chest tightens, making it hard for me to breathe. Why, oh, why isn't she leaving? She should, because I can be cold. I can be a lot of things. But she's new, lonely. Maybe she thinks she's found a kindred spirit. "Virginia," I say finally. "But I've been going to school in New England since I was twelve, so my formative years have been spent here."

Her jaw drops. "You've been in boarding school since you were twelve?"

"Yeah."

"Don't you miss your family?"

"No," I say evenly. "I don't."

"Oh."

I stare at her. Hard. Her own accent rings strange to my ear, but you don't see me asking where she's from or what her family's like. "So why were you spying on me?"

"I wasn't spying!"

"You weren't?"

"No!" she says, and the red blossoming beneath her olive skin pleases me.

I did that.

But the girl keeps going. "I was—I'm *supposed* to be checking the snake traps and making sure there're enough water chestnuts in the back pond for the ecology class. It's part of my work-study hours. But it's sort of scary out here after, you know, what *happened*." She shudders. "Look, I heard a noise. It freaked me out, so I hid. Then I saw you and those guys. . . ."

Her head tilts back. The hazy afternoon sun slides from behind a cloud and strikes her eyes so that I can no longer look directly at her. I glance at my filthy leg instead.

"Aren't you the guy who gets carsick?" she asks.

My shoulders twitch. "Excuse me?"

"On the bus, on the way to the Danby meet, last Wednesday. You had all sorts of patches and wristbands on. You looked like a mummy."

"Like a *mummy*? Really? That's charming. Thank you."

More red blooms. A full bouquet. "I—I didn't mean . . . well, couldn't you just take medicine or something?"

No, I think.

"Why?" I ask.

"I don't know. It just looked kind of ridiculous and like a lot of trouble—"

I cock an eyebrow at her. "I won, didn't I?"

She sighs. I doubt she likes how this is going any more than I do. "Well, now you know why I was hiding in the bushes. What are you doing all the way out here?"

All the way. There's a longing in her voice. Her brown-eyed gaze flicks across the snaking river. We're a good mile from the covered bridge leading back to school grounds. Two miles from the row of white clapboard dorms.

She doesn't trust me.

Good.

It's better that way.

"I think you've got a handle on what I was doing," I tell her. "Seeing as you were watching me and all."

This helps. She puts her hands on those narrow hips, trying to look tough, and I know she's pissed, but come on. The laws of nature don't work like that. I'm a foot taller than her.

Among other things.

"Don't worry," she says. "It won't happen again. You're not that interesting."

"Agreed."

She stomps onto the trail a few yards away, small legs so close to breaking into a run. The need to flee is held captive in every muscle. But she gives me one more glance.

"Hey, Win?" she asks.

Don't. Please don't say my name. You have no idea who I really am.

"Yeah?"

"What're you going to do now?"

"I was thinking about washing my leg off in the river."

She snorts.

"What?" I ask.

"It's like you don't even care someone was killed out here."

I do the shrug thing again because she's right. It's like I don't care. But she's also wrong, because I do.

chapter
two

antimatter

I don't remember my sister's birth, but I've studied the photographs long enough to know she came at midday, greeted by the winter sun streaming through the south-facing windows of my parents' bedroom. My older brother, Keith, appeared with the sunrise, as a sliver of gray dawn began its quiet march across the vast Virginia sky. Me, on the other hand, I was born at night. Like a secret.

As the story goes, I didn't care for Siobhan. My parents introduced me to this pink rooting thing when she was just moments old. I watched her suckle from the place I'd recently been pushed away from, saw the doting eyes of my mother, and I hated her.

My parents threw a christening party not long after. I've studied those photographs, too. More digital proof of my loss. There's Keith and me squeezed into navy suits and forced to stand together at the front of the church. I was three then, still soft and wretched in the way most babyish things are. At seven, my brother stretched taller, stringier. My elongated twin. In the photos, our matching red-brown hair is parted neatly, like a crisp statement of accounts. I'm smiling at the camera. He is not.

After the service, lots of family gathered back at our house. Years later, Keith liked to tell me how starved for attention I was that day, as if my neediness were something to joke about. According to him, I threw myself at relative after relative, hoping to be scooped up, loved, only to be knocked aside again and again. Eventually I hid inside a linen closet and waited for someone to notice my absence. Nobody did. Keith found me hours later when he went looking for extra hand towels to put in the powder room.

Don't worry, I came to love my sister. In fact, I may have loved her most of all, though I never said that out loud. But she knew. I thrilled her. I'd hide and she'd look everywhere for me, her hopeful voice echoing throughout the house as she ran and called out, "Drew! Drew!" Then I'd try to scare her. My heart beat very fast and cool prickles of delight ran up my spine every time I leapt from the shadows and made her scream.

Keith was different, kind where I was brazen. Shortly after that incident at the club with Soren Nichols, we walked to school together. Charlottesville fall, the air still hung with humidity, but the light was changing, becoming more distant, more diffuse. The seasonal fade merged with the wave of darkness rippling in the wake of what I'd done. Everywhere I went, I heard the whispers. I saw the looks. I simply steeled my gaze and perfected an outer shell that promised I was more snob than outcast.

The private school my brother and I attended sat about a mile from our large estate home, a winding tree-lined stroll through one of the city's most prestigious neighborhoods. That morning, Keith's friend Lee leaned out the window of a black Mercedes as his mom drove past and asked Keith if he needed a ride.

"No, thanks!" shouted Keith as he kept his eyes on me, a small smile pulling on his lips. "I'm walking with Drew today." I kept my head down, staring at my ugly black loafers and pressed khaki pants. Severe motion sickness meant I wasn't allowed to ride the bus. Or get in anyone's car. My father said I had an inner ear defect. My mother said I'd outgrow it.

"I don't want you following me," I said loudly. Keith was thirteen. Walking into school with him was sure to bring a crowd of giggling females over toward us. Inevitably I would get teased or babied in some way that offended me. This would lead to throwing punches and an extra trip to the therapist Soren's parents insisted I see in return for not pressing charges. Such a waste, I thought. I'd easily mastered the art of sand tray play and sullen silence.

"I don't want to follow you, either," Keith said. "So you think we could just walk together? Side by side? We don't even have to talk if you don't want to."

"Well . . ."

"Well, what?"

"What if I say no?"

"No what?"

"No, you can't walk beside me."

"Well, then I'd be following you. And, you know, you already asked me not to do that. So unless you'd prefer to follow me . . ."

I glared.

He tried changing the subject. "You looking forward to Christmas this year?"

"Sure, I guess."

"What are you going to ask Santa for?"

It was *October*. I scowled some more. "Santa's not real, you jerk. Don't treat me like some little kid."

"You're nine, Drew. You are a little kid."

He was teasing, but I didn't know he was testing me, too. Losing the belief in Santa Claus was an important developmental milestone. When one can no longer believe in such alluring magic, then rationality has beaten back one's wide-eyed innocence. For most kids, this milestone means a lot.

For my brother, it meant everything.

chapter
three

matter

I stand before the steaming vats of food with a book beneath
one arm and do the math inside my head. It's complicated and
my feet shuffle, trying to get me to leave. Departure is tempt-
ing; I'm tired and not hungry and I'm like this close to my goal
of 6 percent body fat. But I'm also in season. Coach Daniels is
already on my case. I can't just *starve*.

When I've organized my dinner down to the gram, I leave
the kitchen and step into the dining hall. It's like hitting a land
mine because the place is a war zone. Bright lights and human
noise fray my nerves. Pieces of food lie strewn about like casu-
alties. Waffle fries, cornbread, sheet cake, olive slices that re-
semble eyes, even a scattering of chicken bones have been

ground into the thin carpet and tracked across the room. Disgusting. I've never figured out why a school that values tradition as much as ours can't be bothered to teach its students basic *manners*. And God forbid anyone might clear their own tray every now and then. The only time it's even halfway civilized around here is Sunday evenings, when the faculty eats with us. That's when we knot our ties and wear good shoes and the girls are forbidden to bare arms.

I clench my jaw and hold my head high as I walk to an empty table in the far corner by the windows overlooking the playing fields. If my arrogance doesn't drive others away, the fact that I keep my nose buried in Faust certainly will. I could sit with the other runners, but I'm team captain this year. Distance is good. Separation of authority, it keeps the natural order of things.

I sit. Eat. Read.

"Hey."

I tense but don't look up. I know that voice.

"Hey, Teddy."

He slides across from me, a narrow reed. Something's wrong. He's twitchier than usual, blue eyes bouncing around behind wire-rimmed glasses and skinny fingers pattering across the tabletop.

"I saw you," he blurts out.

"You saw me?"

His nose quivers and the moles on his face look like Dalmatian spots. He's that pale. He inches his body toward mine.

"*You* know," he says in a tone that's supposed to sound serious. "This morning. You were by the bridge when the cops were down there. Doing their investigation thing."

"Was I?" In fact I was, but I make it a rule not to reveal any detail about myself without good cause.

"Come on, Win. If you know something, spill it. They said

an animal killed that guy. Whatever it was, it's probably still out there."

"It probably is," I echo. The rumors about an animal in the nearby woods have been whispered all over campus ever since that hiker was found dead out there, although the school hasn't made an official announcement. The guy was a townie, not a student. Technically, they don't have to say anything, but my gut says they'll address the matter eventually. It's an issue of public safety. Of course, it's not a forest animal that *I'm* concerned with, but I did overhear a cop say the guy went missing weeks ago. *Weeks.* Now I can't help but wonder if it happened during the last full moon.

The back of my neck tingles.

Now I can't help but wonder if *I* had something to do with it.

"Winston," Teddy says, leaning closer. He wants to intimidate me.

I stare back. We lock eyes and I don't move. Not a goddamn muscle.

It works. Teddy slumps in an act of submission, like a dog rolling on its back. But let's face it, I'm not his alpha male and we both know it.

"I can't find Lex," he whines. "He's missing. I've looked everywhere."

Lex. Of course. That's what this is about.

"He's not missing," I say. "I saw him this afternoon." Unfortunately I didn't see him until *after* he shoved me in the back while I was pissing into the river. I think he took pictures of me, too. By now he's probably uploaded them onto the Internet and is trying to register me as a sex offender.

"You're sure?" Teddy asks, and right then one of the cooks comes out and shouts that they're closing in five and would we mind making sure there are precisely six chairs at every table. I shake my head. I can't imagine what he's thinking when he says this. An MMA event has broken out, right in the middle of the floor, complete with thundering body slams and flying furniture. It'll be a plus if the chairs just make it through in one piece. But, hey, shoot for the stars, as my dad used to say.

Sssnap!

In a flash, the past comes over me—

getoverheredrew

—and then it's gone, then it's taken a part of me with it. Sweat gathers on my brow. I turn back to Teddy, and I don't think he's noticed, but I feel dark. I feel used.

"I'm absolutely sure," I tell him. "I absolutely saw Lex."

"Yeah, well, he didn't show up for band practice. He's not in his room, either. I just checked."

"So what's your point?"

"My point is that the guy they found was . . ." Teddy licks his lips. "Lex knew him."

"How?"

"He was at that party last year. You know the one I'm talking about."

"I do?"

"Yes. I recognized his picture on the news. The dead guy and his friend, they were *there* that night. At the Rite of Spring. I'm sure of it. Lex talked to them before he went back to the dorms and, you know—"

"Right," I say quickly, because I do know what he's talking about and because I don't want to reminisce about the time Lex Emil OD'd. Not again. He was my roommate for two years, and last April I saved his life. In return he's made mine a living hell. "Well, what are you worried about? He's fine."

Teddy shakes his head. "He's different this year, Win. I can't talk to him like I used to. He's drinking again. Way too much."

I push away the queasy stitch that feels like guilt. I'm good at that by now. "Why are you telling me this? He hates me."

"It's not hate! Lex just—"

"Look, I don't think you have to worry about Lex's well-being unless he plans on roaming around the woods at night by himself."

Teddy's laugh is genuine. "That sounds *exactly* like something Lex would do."

"He'll be fine. Him knowing that guy, it's a total coincidence. This is a small town, after all." I leave the words unspoken, but the implication in my tone is *and you should know*. And he should, because Teddy's not like the rest of us. He's a day student, not a boarder. Meaning he's a townie, too.

Teddy's staring at my plate, what's left of my food, and he's no longer twitchy. He removes his glasses and rubs his eyes. "Hey, Win, you don't still, you know, hurt yourself, do you?"

"No," I say, and I stay very calm, but inside I'm shaken. Yes, he's seen my marks and bruises in the past, but he has no right to ask me something so personal. None. This school devours privacy, and rumors are like drops of blood in an ocean full of predators. So while I like Teddy in an easy kind of way, I can't go there and confess my sins to him. I *won't*. I mean, he's Lex's best friend, and if there's one thing I know, when it comes to humiliating me, Lex Emil is always down for chumming.

chapter
four

antimatter

When you've been kept caged in the dark, it's impossible to see the forest for the trees. It's impossible to see anything, really. Not without bars.

That's what that Charlottesville fall was like, the one where I was nine and could still use my real name without fear. Back then I missed everything, even the most obvious clues, trapped as I was in a head filled with bleak and violent urges. So when Keith returned home from school one afternoon all worked up about animal rights, I felt more lost than enlightened.

Playoff baseball blared on the television. Our father sank torpedo deep in his den chair, Braves cap on, beer in hand, work tie still hanging around his neck like a noose. From my position on the carpeted floor, I sensed more than saw him. His presence loomed large, all shadows and chill. I'd inherited his long nose and severe expression. His dark, dark moods.

Dad held a tenured position at the university. I barely had words for what he did, but I knew it was important. And stressful. Phrases like "climate change," "developing nations," and "actuarial calculations" got thrown around when people talked about him. He traveled frequently. Drank even more frequently.

I dangled a piece of freeze-dried liver over our dog's snout. Pilot was a collie, purebred and from impeccable lineage. At least that's what I'd been told, and it's what I liked to believe. He'd flown to us on a plane as a puppy, all the way from Ireland, which was where my mother grew up. I wanted him to play dead, so I tried using the treat to lure him onto his side. My father threw me a scornful look. I put my hand down.

"Get over here, Drew," he said.

I didn't move. "Huh?"

Dad's eyes remained glued to the flat screen, but he patted the arm of his chair. "Get over here. I want to hear all about how you're going to beat Midgins in the Fall Classic."

"Well, I—I'm not sure if I'm p-playing," I said, although I was sure. The tourney was next weekend and my coach hadn't even brought it up. Not after Soren. No way. I couldn't be trusted.

"*What?*"

I went to stroke Pilot, but I was too rough. My fingers tangled in his fur. He yelped.

"I just m-mean that I'm—"

"Hey, did you know," Keith piped up in a singsong voice, "that animals have rights, too?"

"Like the right to vote?" My father glanced over to where Keith sat on the couch with homework spread all around him. Then he took a long swallow of beer. On the television, someone

sang the national anthem in a warbling voice. Miles of patri-
otic bunting lay draped around the ballpark like a military
funeral.

My brother kept going. "How about the right not to be ex-
ploited or tortured for our consumption?"

"Christ, Keith, where the hell is this coming from?"

"You're being condescending!"

"No, I'm not. I just want to know where you're getting these
ideas."

Keith made a loud huff. "Lee did a presentation at school
today about the living conditions at poultry farms. He showed
video clips of how the chickens are treated. It's disgusting. Beyond disgusting, Dad. It's bad enough to raise these animals
solely for slaughter, but to keep them in those cages their entire
lives, shooting them full of hormones . . ." He went on like this
for a while. Dad nodded along as the Braves took the field, but
I knew what he was thinking: *Thanks a lot, Lee.* Lee lived next
door. He and Keith had struck up a friendship when Lee's family
moved in three years earlier. His family was Jewish, which
still mattered in Charlottesville, but lucky for Lee, our family
looked down on everybody—especially bigots—so we didn't
hold it against him. But he was a fat kid who hated all things
physical, which meant he hated me. I decided right then and
there that whatever stance Lee was taking on this whole animal rights thing, I was of the opposite view. Just because.

I held out the dog treat again. Pilot picked his head up.

"So let me get this straight," my father rumbled. "You don't
object to the actual consumption of animals, right?"

Keith hesitated. "Right."

"It's how the animals are treated before they're slaughtered
that bothers you? Not the actual slaughtering."

"I guess."

"So the predator should respect the life of its prey? Am I

understanding you? The lion should honor the zebra? It should feel empathy?"

Now Keith looked furious. He *was* being condescended to. It happened all the time. Mom called it "the Socratic method" and said it was the way Dad lectured and the reason he could get so many people to see things his way. She also said it never paid to make him mad, but Keith seemed immune to the whole thing. Or more like allergic. "You know that's not what I mean. We're not animals. We're *human*. We have certain responsibilities—"

"We're not what?" My father grinned, but he didn't look happy. His face took on an eerie cast from the glow of the television. A major league leer. I shuddered.

Keith shot a nervous glance in my direction. "Empathy's not a bad thing, Dad."

"Really? Are you so sure? Even when it's a matter of life or death?"

"That's not what I'm talking about."

"Then what exactly are you talking about?"

"God!" Keith exclaimed. "Am I the only one around here who gives a crap about anything but myself?"

I tensed and waited for my father's reaction. Even *I* didn't like Keith's tone.

But nothing happened.

After a moment, Keith dropped his gaze. "I mean, how hard would it be just to buy free-range chicken from now on?" he muttered. "'Cause that would be a great start."

"Free-range?" My dad gave a sharp bark of laughter, startling me. Pilot growled. The sound came from deep in his belly, and I buried my face in his snowy ruff. Inhaled his doggy scent.

"Free-range," he repeated. "Hell, sure, Keith. *That* we can do."

I growled, too.

My dad swatted the arm of his chair one more time.

"Get over here, Drew."

chapter
five

matter

The directive is handed down the following morning: We're
not allowed in the back woods on the far side of the river anymore. This is expected and I'm not sure what took so long, but
the entire student body is complaining and making idiotic argu-
ments like how there's a greater chance of dying in a dorm fire
than being eaten by a wild animal so maybe we should all strip
naked, cover ourselves in fire-retardant foam, and sleep in the
parking lot.

You know, just in case.

But the headmaster is firm. There's something out there, he
tells us while we're all crammed shoulder to shoulder and thigh
to thigh in the dark shadows of the school's creaking chapel. A

bear. A cougar. A wolf in sheep's clothing. No one knows. State wildlife experts will investigate. The matter should be resolved quickly, and our cooperation is appreciated.

The platitudes and clichés spill from his mouth in rapid succession like the lame script of some poorly programmed android. I listen but learn nothing new. I do know the cops are in the woods again this morning. I know because I watched them trudge out there, real early, with their cadaver dogs and everything. But today's forecast calls for rain, and this will wash away evidence, I guess. That's too bad. I'd like the truth to be known as much as the next person.

More, really.

I feel restless. I do math inside my head. It's been twenty-five days since the last full moon. That was during the first week of school, back in September, and I spent that night like others before it. I walked in the dark, alone. At curfew, I returned to my room, where I tossed and turned for hours. When I finally slept, I awoke to failure. I hadn't changed. Again. Or so I thought.

Now I don't know what to think.

I fidget. I long to leave. My elbow hurts and my hip hurts because I'm curled against the end of a pew, doing everything I can to avoid letting Brandon Black breathe on me. He smells awful, like some combination of scrambled eggs and designer body spray, and I have to inhale through my mouth because I'm this close to puking my guts all over the scuffed wood planks beneath my feet. I wrench my head to the right, and in an ocean of J. Crew and American Eagle, I spy the girl who looks like a boy sitting across the aisle and one row back. She's wearing cargo shorts and leather sandals.

She's also staring directly at me.

I nod. Her ears go red and she quickly faces forward. I follow her gaze. She's not looking at the headmaster, I don't think.

She's focused on what's behind him—the Gothic wood carving that hangs above the altar. Supposedly, a group of students made it over a hundred years ago, back when the school was all girls. It's dedicated to the founding headmistress. She's the one who rescued this tiny clapboard chapel from demolition and had it moved piece by piece all the way up the mountain and reconstructed on the campus grounds. As the story goes, each girl chiseled a specific letter, one at a time. It must have taken them forever because the thing is *huge*. Today it's kept well oiled, a massive mahogany glow that serves as the backdrop of every gathering we have in here, and although the school is secular, the quote is from Corinthians. It's meant to be sacred, but it's really just stupid.

Love never faileth?

Yeah, right.

chapter

six

antimatter

This I *really* didn't understand.

Our family was cultured. If and when we traveled, we spent our days visiting museums and galleries, our nights in theaters or lecture halls. We didn't *do* rural. Which was why it didn't make sense that an entire Saturday in late November had been set aside to visit Semper Liberi, a hokey-sounding animal preserve located in West Virginia.

What I *did* understand was that it was a good two-and-a-half-hour drive to the place—a twisty ride that would take us into the depths of the Monongahela National Forest. I didn't want to go, for numerous reasons. Besides the obvious car dilemma, I did not enjoy zoos or aquariums or anything related.

The animals always smelled or hid, and I generally just didn't care. But I had no say in the matter.

I survived the road trip in the family Volvo by skipping breakfast and getting drugged up on Phenergan, the only medication with the power to suppress my motion sickness. It also knocked me out cold. Keith had to shake me awake as we pulled into the parking lot of the preserve. I flailed and tried to hit him. I wanted to continue sleeping. I wanted to remain unwoken.

I stepped from the car into the frigid autumn air. A huge puddle of drool smeared across my cheek and all the way down my neck. The echo of familiar nightmares rattled in my head, and my limbs felt weak and unreliable. I lagged behind my family, shadowed by the crunch of gravel beneath my feet and lost in my own internal fog. A bitter wind howled off the hillside with locomotive force and I stumbled, once, twice, over the untied laces of my Nikes. But I caught myself. Kept going.

Nothing looked real. Nothing felt right.

I heard my name bounce around in the breeze like a Wilson double core on clay and looked to see Keith beckoning me with one arm. My brother smiled calmly, a beatific look. He stood at a split trailhead with beech and black cherry trees towering above him in their newly bare autumn glory.

"Come on!" he called.

"Why are we here?"

"Come on," he repeated. "We're going to see the wolves."

We took the left-hand trail and hoofed it down into the dark woods. The sharp scent of birch oil hung in the air. My brother's body fairly thrummed with excitement, and I struggled to keep up. I was no match for his long legs or bright-eyed eagerness.

"You all right?" He ducked down once to squint at me. His red-brown hair flopped over his forehead, and he'd recently taken to wearing button-down shirts that reminded me of our father's favorite students. The ones who stopped by our house to drink with him at all hours of the night. The ones our mother hated.

"I'm fine," I mumbled, although this wasn't quite true. Phenergan residue left me with a pounding headache and dry mouth, like playground sand, which I sometimes ate. "What did you say about wolves?"

"They have them here at the sanctuary. Pretty cool, huh?" Keith jutted his chin in the direction of our parents. "It took forever to convince them to bring us. You know how Dad is with the whole animal rescue thing. I had to promise to get straight A's and not convert you into a vegetarian, but I wanted you to see it."

So Keith had been to this place before? And coming again had been his idea? That was news to me. He shouldn't have bothered. I was in no danger of becoming a vegetarian.

We caught up with the rest of our family, and an overly friendly docent waved us into the visitors center. Siobhan immediately set to work on being hyper. She jumped up and down in an imitation of Tigger on a sugar high, and the movement made her ribboned pigtails bounce like mattress springs. Our mother, who had little in the way of patience, told her to stop about twenty times. When the docent launched into a boring speech about the history and mission of the preserve, I crept up from behind, took one of Siobhan's honey-colored curls into my hand, and tugged.

"Hey, you," I whispered. I hoped my sister would smile or squeal the way she always did when I got too close. She didn't. Instead my father warned, "Drew!" and I slunk off to the far side of the room, where my stomach growled and hot beads of resentment welled up inside my chest.

Cruising the back wall like a lowrider, I stared at the

wildlife photography hanging above me. There was a bobcat. Birds of prey. A family of raccoons. A big-eared thing I thought was a rat until I read the sign informing me it was a fennec fox. Then I came to the wolves. Such ugly beasts. All scary eyes and open mouths and lolling tongues. What was so cool about them? Sure, I'd absorbed their gothic draw from books I read. Movies I watched. Wolves were meant to be fearsome, wild, the darkness untamed. I'd met the lone wolf. The big bad wolf. The wolf at the door. I'd cried wolf, wolfed down my food, and thrown others to the wolves when at all possible.

I stared harder.

The longer I stood there, the more their predatory gaze felt familiar, chillingly so.

I thought of the look in Soren's eyes before I hit him. My father's words on empathy.

My head swam.

What was I? Hunter or hunted?

My stomach growled again.

When the talk ended, we got to tour the property. The animals kept here couldn't be returned to the wild for some reason or another. As I stepped down into the preserve, the first thing I noticed was the stench. Everything everywhere smelled strongly of animal waste. A wooden placard told us that the first enclosure we came upon housed a herd of miniature goats and a donkey. Siobhan waggled her fingers and stuffed blades of grass through the fence into the waiting mouth of a speckled kid.

I wandered off on my own. Kept going until my family was out of sight. I passed the little fox and the raptors until I reached the wolf habitat. The animals all lounged in the dirt, lazy. Staring at them, I felt disappointed, romance swallowed up by reality. They weren't even big. More like exotic dogs. I remembered the guide telling us the current pack consisted of a young male,

his mate, and an older female whose mate died over the summer. That made me sad. Wolves mated forever, he'd said, so that
meant the older wolf would be alone until she died. I wondered
if she knew. I thought I understood how she might feel.

I turned and kept walking.

Above me, the sun struggled to break through the thick
cover of tree branches and I shivered in my unlined jacket.
With a twist of my head, I caught a faint view of the surrounding mountain range and the wide swath of river chewing through
the land below. My heart pounded from the quiet beauty. I
wanted it to take me. I wanted it to fill me up, this cool flush of
green and brown forest sanctuary.

Heading deeper and deeper into the West Virginia woods, I
realized I was not alone. The older wolf had followed me, pushing through the underbrush not three feet from the path where
I walked. I swiveled to look at her. Amber eyes bored straight
into mine. Her ears flattened. She was a ratty beast, with
patches of thinning fur and protruding bones.

Her presence pleased me, but I couldn't have said why.
Maybe she was drawn to our joint loneliness. I walked to a
cutout in the cyclone fencing meant for cameras and fished one
of Pilot's dog treats from my pocket. Then I thrust my hand
through the chain-link barrier.

"Come here, girl," I crooned. I made a kissing sound with
my lips.

The wolf took one step forward, then squatted to pee in the
soil. She didn't take her eyes off me. A dozen more steps and we
stood facing each other, separated by mere inches. Her coat
was a dull swirl of brown, silver, and white. I wanted desper-
ately to touch her and reached out farther with the hand that
held the small piece of liver. It happened in an instant. She
whirled and slashed with her sharp teeth and I flinched, dropping the treat in the process. The wolf snapped it up, then

vanished. My cheeks burned. I pulled my arm back and glanced around.

No one else had seen a thing.

Later, we ate lunch at a roadhouse across the highway from the preserve. It was a giant wooden structure full of dusty nooks and crannies and a sparsely populated bar. My father drank quietly while NASCAR played on about eight different television screens. I was starving. My mother admonished me not to eat too much, but I ate my entire burger and finished Siobhan's, too, when she passed it to me under the table. Afterward, Keith and I slipped away and snuck up a rickety staircase to the second floor, where we discovered an air hockey table and an old jukebox. The only song I recognized was Don Ho's "Tiny Bubbles."

The Phenergan didn't work on the ride back. My sleep was fitful and in my dreams I saw the old wolf, her yellow gaze and the points of her teeth. Even she hated me. I was worthless. My eyes flew open when we were about halfway home and I vomited suddenly with a groan and a rush. Siobhan screamed and held her nose. I started to cry. We pulled over at the next gas station and Keith helped me change my shirt and tried to comfort me.

"It's okay, Drew," he said, and tousled my hair. I kept sobbing and hiccuping. I could feel my father's disapproval, my mother's disdain. I knew I could only be falling short in their eyes.

"I hate myself."

"Don't say that."

"I want to die."

Keith put an arm around me. "No, no, you don't. Okay, kid? Just believe me when I say, someday life is going to get a lot better. I promise."

"How do you know?"

"I just know. Soon you'll know, too."

chapter

seven

matter

While everyone else is busy bitching or gossiping or spilling fake tears over the dead townie, I slip from the chapel into muggy morning air that's way too warm for this time of year. It feels like autumn's missed its stop or had to reschedule because I'm already sweating bullets.

In the slowly dispersing crowd of three hundred or so other students, I can't see where the dark-haired girl has gone. I don't go out of my way to find her, but it kind of bothers me that she was staring like that.

What was she looking for?

And more important, what did she see?

I trot beneath a line of weary birch trees over to Hudson

House, the third-year dorm. My dorm. Once inside, I make a beeline for the communal bathroom. It's deserted, so after I use the toilet and wash my hands, I peer at myself in the mirror for a long time, examining things like the size of my eyes and the size of my teeth and the way my ribs show through my skin. I'm looking for answers, I guess, but I don't find them. I do find I need a haircut. My hair falls across my eyes in a way that's rakish when I squint but sloppy when I don't. Once, when I was a freshman, a senior girl called me cute, but people usually say I look intense. A lot of times they ask why I don't smile, which I hate. No one wants to answer that question.

Ever.

Trust me on that.

Leaving the bathroom, I run smack into Donnie Lipman. I literally run into him. Good thing I'm tall or I'd have a face full of chest hair and polo shirt. Instead it's shoulder against shoulder, like two bucks in rut, and Donnie and I jump back at the same time. He's got the single next to mine, and he listens to dubstep and trance music all day and all night, which means I do, too. Donnie doesn't like me. The feeling's mutual, of course, but I stop him anyway.

"Hey, what's the name of that new girl?" I ask. "The junior transfer."

I get a tight nod in return as Donnie pointedly avoids eye contact. "That the chick Channer's trying to bang?"

Blake Channer plays goalie for the ice hockey team, which can't be right, so I shake my head.

He shrugs. "That's the only junior transfer I know. Redhead. Cute ass, kind of a butterface."

Definitely not her. I turn and walk away from Donnie, straight down the hall, straight into my room. I'm lucky. I have a corner single with lots of windows. It should feel like an aerie in the trees, but today I'm reminded of gallows. Today I'm reminded of impending doom. My hands shake as I close the door.

Breathe, I tell myself, but it's not that easy. I'm filled too tight with this sharp sting-stab of guilt.

Or is it shame?

I don't always know the difference.

The thin white curtains are pulled wide open. I spy other students walking on the path below. They are out there. I am in here. Even though it's what I wanted, it feels wrong not having a roommate this year. I'm used to having a second nervous system in my living space. Something to distract me when my mind rockets off on a tangent like it is now. Someone to keep me grounded.

Inhale through the nose, I tell myself. *Exhale through the mouth.*

As usual, I don't want to think about Lex or why I live alone these days, and I really don't want to think about *her,* so I pace the hardwood floor once, twice. I pass a bed, a desk, a chair, a dresser, a shelf full of books, a pile of dirty clothes, a pile of clean ones. It takes eighteen steps a lap. It takes 4.2 seconds. I think I could die in 4.2 seconds if I jumped from the proper height or used the proper weapon.

In fact, I know I could.

Damn. I turn and fumble for my backpack. I need to get out of here. Like *now.* This breathing thing is going nowhere fast, like world peace and those predictions of the Rapture. Besides, I've got things to do. Information to find.

I need to understand what's happening to my own body.

And it's not like I've got all the time in the world.

I move with newfound purpose. I'm heading to the school's science library, located in the biology lab. There are books there I can check out. Ones that might help. And now's a good time to go—morning classes have been canceled so students can "jointly process the emotional impact of the tragedy." But as I hustle across campus toward the tight cluster of academic buildings, it's clear this has been interpreted as a euphemism for "smoking weed together behind the gym." Whatever. I just keep walking.

Maybe the callousness of using someone's death as an excuse to get high should shock me, but it doesn't. We're reading *A Clockwork Orange* right now in English, and just last week Mrs. Villanova told us about the "moral holiday" period in adolescent brain development. I guess it's the time nature sets aside for us to raise holy hell and not give a crap about anyone else. Only I'm not buying it, because I don't think it's a phase. Except maybe the holiday part, and that's more about being too stupid to cover your tracks than true values. From what I can tell, morality is a word. Nothing more. There're the things people do when others are watching and the things we do when they aren't. I'd like to believe Anthony Burgess knew that, but then that dumb last chapter of his book went and ruined the whole thing. That made me mad, and so I think the movie version got it right: people don't change. Their nature, that is. There are other kinds of change, of course.

Like physical change.

Stepping into the science building, I catch sight of Mr. Byles, the chemistry teacher, standing in the hallway. He's talking to another student, but I know he sees me by the way he squares his shoulders, military sharp. Over the summer I grew taller than him, and apparently I'm not the only one who's noticed.

"Win," he says as the other student scampers off. "How are you doing?"

I'm not a great scholar by any stretch, but I excel in those subjects I find relevant and worthy of my consideration. Science, I devour. History, I have no use for. But I like Mr. Byles and I've done well in his class, so these are the reasons I hope his inquiry is merely an everyday *how are you doing*. Or an obligatory there's-been-a-tragedy-in-our-midst *how are you doing*. Or even an I'm-not-comfortable-with-death-and-I-want-you-to-reassure-me *how are you doing*. But I absolutely do not want that honeyed hint of concern and condescension in his voice to be personal. I do not want it to be about *me*.

"I'm fine," I say evenly.

"There are counselors available all day. You know, if you want to talk to someone."

I'm sweating again. Why is he saying it like that, all hushed and serious? And why is he staring? He's never looked at me like that before. Last year he practically worshipped the ground I walked on. Last year I was the best student he'd ever taught. The only thing I saw in his eyes back then was envy.

"I don't need to talk to a counselor," I say, a little louder than I intend. My head begins to buzz the way it does when I get overexcited. It's not good for me to get upset.

"Okay," he says.

I hate this. The buzzing grows louder. I am a living hive of dread. The memories, those images I don't want, are swarming around inside me, looking for a way, any way, to get out. . . .

"I need to go," I mumble. "To the biology lab."

"You ever read that article I sent you? About—"

"Sea quarks," I manage feebly. "Yeah, thanks for that."

I know he wants me to stay and talk because that's what we did last year. We talked. Not about my grief or my anger or my guilt over how my siblings died like martyrs cast against my wicked ways. Those are the things I never talk about. No, we talked about matter—most notably quarks, those tiniest possible components of everything. They come in six flavors, you know: up, down, top, bottom, charm, and strange. I'll admit those talks helped me, and when I read about the sea quarks, I understood why. They contain particles of matter and antimatter, and where the two touch exists this constant stream of creation and annihilation. Scientists call this place "the sea," and it's what pitches inside of me as I hurry away from Mr. Byles, ignoring his furrowed brow, his worried frown.

I am of the sea.

I am of instability.

I am of harsh, choppy waves roiling with all the up-ness, down-ness, top-ness, bottom-ness contained within my being.

I am of charm and strange.

Annihilation.

Creation.

Annihilation.

chapter
eight

antimatter

With April came my tenth birthday, and in May Keith turned fourteen. School ended and we all watched Keith graduate from middle school. The small private academy we attended had its own high school right next door, so the transition was more symbolic than anything else. Just another beat in the dark rhythm of our family.

Summer vacation stretched before me. Ten weeks I planned to fill with tennis and the sweet rush of victory. I had no more qualms about playing again. The previous summer's drama with Soren only added to my toolbox of mental strengths; I was scary. This fact filled me with a crawling sort of anticipation, both thrilling and repulsive. I'd run into Soren only once since breaking his jaw. This occurred during a spring clinic at my own club when he'd shown up with his coach. I took one look at the jittery hitch in his serve, the way he bit at his lower lip until it bled, the way he missed every single ball because he was so freaking nervous to run into *me*, and I promptly dropped my racket.

I marched right home, up to my room, and stayed there. I couldn't speak. I couldn't sleep. My mind drifted, teased with morbid images I knew better than to tell anyone about. On the third day, when the sun rose to the sound of chickadees tapping at my window, my dark mood had miraculously vanished. My voice returned.

My killer instinct was back.

But my season of triumph wasn't meant to be. The day after graduation, my parents broke the news: Keith and I were being shipped off, on a train, no less, to spend eight weeks in Concord, Massachusetts—home to Emerson, Thoreau, and my father's parents. Siobhan was too young, so she would stay behind.

I was understandably anxious. My impression of my grandparents was blurry and undefined. I hardly knew them. Plus traveling was a huge deal; I was informed that one wasn't allowed to eat or drink in my grandfather's leather-trimmed Audi, much less barf in it. Tennis was another issue. The fall season was the most competitive, and if I didn't play every day, I would be in no position to maintain my number one ranking. But my biggest concern was homesickness. I couldn't imagine not sleeping in my own bed, with Pilot curled at my feet. I couldn't imagine not being home with Siobhan, who made me feel brave because she so wasn't. Keith understood, though. He'd gone last summer and went out of his way to tell me how much fun we were going to have.

"Why do I have to go?" I sniffled.

"Because Dad'll be gone at that fellowship all summer in New York, and Mom . . . can't."

"Why not?" I asked, although even I knew our mother was prone to her own bouts of blackness, ones where she struggled to eat. Or get out of bed. Or open her eyes.

"She'll have her hands full taking care of Siobhan," Keith said.

"I can take care of myself!"

"You need to get out of here," he said firmly. "We both do, okay? It'll be good for us. A real adventure. Swimming, hiking . . . cousins." Our cousins, we'd see them, too. They lived in nearby Lexington, three of them. All girls.

I appreciated Keith's attitude but remained distraught. Still, there was nothing to be done about it, so on June 24, starved and drugged close to comatose, I boarded an Amtrak heading north with my brother.

From the platform, Siobhan waved and blew kisses at us as we pulled away.

I lifted my head and waved back.

chapter
nine

matter

Common trust. It's the school's one rule.

The only one necessary.

It's the reason there are no locks on the dorm room doors.

It's the reason there are no lockers for our crap.

It's the reason we can borrow books from the library on our own.

It's the reason I can enter the deserted biology lab on a Tuesday morning in October and not feel like a criminal.

I keep the lights off as I go in. The windows are huge, and plenty of sun leaks in to pool around the bookshelves that line the far wall. I pass the massive steel refrigerator that hums and shakes. It holds the fetal pigs from our most recent class, and

I'm tempted to peek at mine. The AP section is small enough and the science budget is large enough that we don't have to partner up, so I've got my very own piglet. It's pink and black. I guess I should say *she's* pink and black, since the first thing we did was record the gender. Then I opened the abdominal cavity, but I still haven't finished with the mouth and neck or removed the heart, so that'll have to happen tomorrow. Thank God for preservatives.

Ouch. Both knees crack as I squat to read the titles on the textbooks, but I quickly find what I'm looking for. Or at least I find the right *kind* of book, because none of them are going to give me the answers I need. Too much of me is a mystery. But maybe I'll find the right questions to ask. *Neuroscience. Biopsychology. Origin of the Species*. There's a book by Ludwig Wittgenstein, too. It's called *Philosophical Investigations*. That doesn't sound like it has anything to do with biology. But I've heard of the guy. I know I have.

I grab it.

My hands tremble as I flip through the pages. The book is made up of short quotes and ideas. The ones my eyes flit across have something to do with rule-following and paradoxes and trying to understand how the hell anyone can ever make sense of someone else's words. That's when I remember what it is I know about Wittgenstein. It has nothing to do with his philosophy. Lex once e-mailed me a link to his Wikipedia page, and idiot that I am, I read it. So this is what I know: Three of Wittgenstein's brothers committed suicide.

Now I really feel ill. I want to lie down for, like, the rest of the decade. But I can't. I put *Philosophical Investigations* back and take the other books over to a desk. There are a few things I need to know. Like how stress can affect the body. Last year in health class, I learned girls sometimes get their periods late when they're under stress. That type of thing doesn't make me

squeamish the way it does other guys, so I'm glad I paid attention when they told us that. Lex sat next to me in class that day
and he couldn't even look at the teacher. Said blood made him
woozy. So instead of listening to the lecture, he put in those
orange foam earplugs, the kind they give you on the airplane
when you want to sleep. Then he stole my notebook and drew
cartoon penises all over the cover in Sharpie along with the
sage message VAGINAS ARE GROCE, which made no sense at all
considering the amount of time he spends online looking at the
things.

I turn back to the textbooks. Well, I know puberty and all
that is regulated by hormones, so I flip to the index of the neuroscience one and find a diagram of the endocrine system that
shows where all the different glands are located in the body. It
makes sense, sort of. But how does the body know *when* to start
changing? Who sets the biological alarm clock? That's what I
want to know, because I think mine is on snooze. I'm *sixteen*.
I've done the part of growing up that means a lower voice and
sticky dreams and hair down there, but those other changes, the
ones that live deeper and darker, the ones I spend all night
waiting for as I lie on my back gazing up at the warm belly of
the moon . . . well, *those* changes haven't happened yet. Or at
least, I don't think they have.

Not unless stress can affect memories, too.

Not unless—

"Winston," a voice says, so close that I can feel a beat of hot
breath against the back of my neck.

I jump.

My instinct controls me.

I see nothing. I feel *everything*.

Sssnap!

*Sunlight leaps off the bridge's metal bracings, blinding me. The sound
of a train whistle blares in my ears. I pull myself halfway onto the rail-*

ing and the wind snaps so hard my shirt is practically torn off. I look down. My legs shake. The water is so far away and I don't want to do this.

I don't want to do this.

ohgodohgodohgod

"Hey! Fucking . . . *stop it!*"

I blink. I'm back. The air smells of bleach and I gag-choke before being able to breathe again. My arms sway like falling Jenga towers. Lex Emil lies pinned beneath me on the lab floor. I'm bigger than him. My knee digs into his scrawny ribs. His round face is blotchy and scratched, with dyed black hair matted across his forehead. His chest heaves in time with the asthmatic rattle of his lungs. He's holding his hands against my shirt, pushing me back. There's fear in his eyes.

I roll off him, stunned. I gag again, an awful sound. I can't help it. These flashes of mine, getting stuck in the past, they're a part of who I am, but I don't think I'll ever get used to them.

"Fuck," Lex says, more to himself than to me. His hands lower. "It's okay. You're okay, right?"

"Yeah."

"You clicked out. You could have killed me."

I shiver. "Yeah."

He crawls to his feet and shakes like a dog leaving water. Then he wags a finger at me, cocky smile flourishing across his face. A gleam of silver above his chin makes me realize he's gotten some kind of new piercing, a labret. It's ugly.

"You could at least try and sound remorseful," he says.

"I'm sorry."

"I seriously doubt that. I mean, I don't blame you, but Christ, you would've lit into anyone just now. You're losing it, Win."

No, I'm not. Something else is happening.

Lex reads my mind. His attention falls upon the books spread out on the lab table, and his eyes widen with understanding.

"What do we have here?" he says.

"I don't know."

He laughs softly. "The beast within, huh? You still waiting?"

I glare.

"Guess you'll know come Friday night, right? That's the full moon?"

"I guess so," I say, because it's true. I will know Friday night. Change is imminent.

It *has* to be.

"Yeah, well, have fun with that," Lex says. "Moon or no moon, I don't plan on being anywhere near you."

"Good," I snarl, and he laughs even harder than before. My hands curl into fists. I want him to shut up.

Lex notices and skitters toward the door.

"Hey, Win," he says as he leaves, "maybe it's your head that's broken, not your body. Ever think about that?"

chapter

ten

antimatter

Keith and I arrived late in the day, only to get whisked from the train station to a stately colonial in the heart of Concord just as the sun began to set. Such a cold home. It smelled like onions. We sat down for dinner right away, but I couldn't eat.

My grandmother glared at my untouched plate. Her long face and silver hair reminded me of an Irish wolfhound. Stern. Chiseled. Focused.

"Is something wrong, Andrew?"

"No, ma'am." I squirmed in my seat and wondered where my grandfather was. He'd vanished after bringing our bags inside. *Poof.* Like a magic trick.

"How's your mother?"

"She's all right. She gets, you know, real tired a lot."

"I just bet she does," my grandmother said smoothly. "Your father says you're playing very well these days."

"Yes."

"He's arranged for you to practice at our club this summer. Every weekday at eight A.M. sharp."

"Yes, ma'am."

"What's your rating?"

I tossed my head. "Four point five."

Her nostrils flared. "And you've atoned for that . . . embarrassing incident last year, I hope."

I knew what she meant. "I guess."

"It made me sick to hear about that. Absolutely sick. Imagine how your father felt to see his son behaving like that."

"Yes, ma'am."

"Like an *animal*."

I stared straight ahead at the orange-and-brown wallpaper lining the dining room and kicked my heels against the chair spindles, over and over. I wished I were an animal. Like a jungle cat. I'd hiss and spit. And maul.

Then up the stairs we went for an early bedtime. Keith and I shared a small room at the back of the house that overlooked a duck pond and a pair of willow trees. I hated it. It didn't even have a television. We changed into our pajamas and brushed our teeth, and then my insides hurt and I wouldn't leave the bathroom because I needed to go but couldn't. Keith heard me whimpering and came in.

"What's wrong, Drew?"

"My tummy hurts."

"Oh, for God's sakes," he groaned.

"What?"

"Look, just don't say 'tummy,' okay? That's a baby word." He led me back down the hall and tucked me into the single bed closest to the window. "You know, this is where Dad and Uncle Kirby grew up."

"It still hurts," I whispered.

"You'll be fine," he said, and I fell asleep.

It didn't last. My eyes cracked open hours later in the black humid heat of the night. Keith snored, and the lack of central air meant my clothes stuck to every part of my body. My empty stomach growled, and I snuck down the back stairs into the kitchen. The stove clock blinked 2:13. I was pretty sure my grandparents were holed up in their bedroom at the front of the house, but I didn't want to risk getting caught. I crept to the refrigerator, pulled out a handful of white bread and sliced turkey, and jammed it all down my throat while standing in the middle of the room. Then I slunk back upstairs, overfull and queasy. I still couldn't sleep. I opened the bedroom window and stuck my head outside. Fireflies glowed around the branches of the willow trees, and a tiny sliver of moon hung high in the sky, surrounded by stars. *The moon.* My heart skipped a beat and tears slid from my eyes, hot, stinging. I didn't want to be here.

Stop it. You're being a baby. Just stop crying already!

Although I had my own bed, I took my shirt off and lay beside Keith. I pressed against him. My heart slowed and my stomach settled. There was something calming in the scent of him, the feel of him. He was familiar.

chapter

eleven

matter

Coach Daniels stands in the parking lot, waving his arms like a monster and yelling for wayward runners to *hurry the hell up* and get on the team bus. Apparently, we need to *get this show on the road right quick and fast* if we want to make it to the cross-country meet on time. I sit back and close my eyes. Yeah, sure, I'm captain, but I don't care if anyone gets left behind. I just don't. All I care about right now is winning. The weekend's taking forever to get here, and I need the distraction. Badly. I need physical torment and the fleeting validation of victory.

"Can I sit with you?" A soft voice breaks into my reverie.

I blink. I look up. It's *her*. The dark-haired girl, the boyish one.

"There are no empty seats," she explains, and she looks about as exasperated as I feel.

I oblige, of course, because I can't exactly say no, and as I slide toward the window, the doors close and the bus's engine roars to life.

"Thanks." The girl settles beside me. She places her gym bag between us like a wall.

I give a half shrug like her presence is no big deal, but in truth, I'm put out. I still have no clue why she was looking at me like that in the chapel the other day. And I still don't like that she did it.

At least now I know her name.

It's *Jordan*.

She turns to me, kind of frowning, and my insides ball up. *God*. Last time we talked she said I wasn't interesting; I repelled her. But something's changed. Something's different. Maybe she can sense my instability. Maybe she can feel the heat of destruction flaring inside me, that subatomic sea of flame and fallout.

Maybe she *knows*.

The bus draws forward, inching into the street.

"Win," Jordan says, and my heart sort of stutters.

"Yeah?"

"I wanted to tell you thanks for backing me up in civics class last week. During the immigration debate."

"No problem," I say, but I remain edgy. What an odd thing to mention.

She leans in, fingering the gold cross that hangs from a chain around her neck and lowering her voice. "It's just, a lot of my family, they're from Mexico, you know? So some of the things that were being said, well, they bothered me."

I give a quick nod. "They bothered me, too."

"Yeah?" She stares. "I guess I thought . . . I just figured you'd think differently, that's all."

I don't know how to respond.

Jordan points. "You've got those wrist thingies on again."

This is true. "What about them?"

"Well, you're not going to get sick, are you?"

I tense. I mean, what kind of question is that? Like my body is mine to master.

"If I do, you'll be the first to know," I say stiffly.

Her head tilts. "Is that supposed to be a joke?"

Confused, I stare a little shamelessly at her. Jordan doesn't seem to mind. She pulls something out of her gym bag. A wrinkled study sheet of what appears to be Latin conjugations.

"Classes are hard here," she tells me as she tries flattening the paper against her knee. It looks like a lost cause.

"Are they?"

"Compared to my public school, absolutely. I have to actually, like, study. It sucks."

"Ad astra per aspera," I say.

Jordan looks up. "That's Latin, huh? What does it mean?"

" 'To the stars through difficulty.' It's the school motto."

She snorts. "Well, the most difficult thing around here is meeting people. Is there a motto for that?"

"Probably."

Jordan leans closer. Close enough for me to smell her. "I mean, finding a seat on the bus shouldn't be such a struggle, right? It's got to be me, though. My own roommate ditches me to go home every weekend, back to New York." She sighs. "You're like the only person around here who'll talk to me, Win. Even if you do your best not to."

Is she being serious? I don't know and I don't ask. Withdrawal's a reflex for me, a protective one, like quill raising or those spiders that throw hairs. I scoot away from Jordan. As far away as possible. Our uniforms are sleeveless and my bare shoulder presses hard against the bus's cool metal siding while I suck in autumn air rushing through the open window.

I fix my gaze on the horizon and keep it there. Cider stands, corn mazes, pumpkin patches, all whip by at Mach speed. Even the moon is visible, very faint, a chalky smudge in the clear blue sky. It teases as always, with its shape and its secrets, but I feel closer than I ever have.

Soon, my mind whispers.

Very soon.

chapter
twelve

antimatter

We met up with our cousins on the third day. These were the daughters of my father's younger brother and they lived in neighboring Lexington. Our grandparents kept their photographs plastered all over the house, and Keith schooled me on their names and ages: Anna was sixteen, Charlotte, fourteen, and Phoebe was eleven. I didn't know them. Apparently, they'd visited us before, in Charlottesville, when I was younger, but I didn't remember any of that. I didn't remember a lot of things. Sometimes I wondered if my mind had been scrubbed clean of certain memories like in that weird movie with Jim Carrey. But if that was the case, why didn't I just get a whole new life where

I wouldn't be reminded of the fact I'd forgotten things in the first place?

Keith, on the other hand, had a flawless memory. Photographic, his teachers sometimes boasted, but Keith said it wasn't anything good to have so much stuff stuck inside his brain. "It's too crowded in there," he told me. "I don't have room to think."

We left the house early that afternoon and weaved through the summer crowds. Every day Concord crawled with hordes of travelers and tour buses that double-parked and shimmered in the New England heat. I didn't like it, which was weird. The visitors bothered me even though I was a tourist, too.

Once we were out of the downtown maze of streets, my eyes stayed glued to the ground. Something in the stone slabs beneath my feet glittered and sparkled like diamonds. It felt like walking on the surface of a distant planet. Foreign. Unknowable. We entered the wrought-iron gates of the old town cemetery. Keith cleared his throat. I looked up and there they were. The girls. All three of them.

They lounged on beach towels in the prickly grass, amid chipped slate headstones and faded American flags. Keith smoothed out his shirt and walked straight up to Charlotte (she went by Charlie) and declared: "You've changed."

She didn't squeal the way girls at home did when they sat in groups and Keith talked to them. Instead, Charlie crossed her legs and arched her back. Long red hair pooled over one shoulder. I thought she looked mean, vixen sly, but Keith wouldn't take his eyes off her.

"You're right," she said finally. "I have."

"Why didn't you write back when I e-mailed you?"

She leaned to one side and shot me a quizzical look. "How old is he?"

Keith twisted around. I sat a few feet away on a stone bench with my arms folded. The last thing I wanted to do was sit and listen to them talk all day. What I *did* want was to play tennis, but it was Sunday. I couldn't go until tomorrow.

Keith turned back to Charlie. "He's ten."

"He looks older."

I smiled. This was a common misconception because of my height. People sometimes thought I was twelve or thirteen. I'd even been called a brute.

Keith just shrugged and pushed his bangs from his eyes. Charlie held out her hand and wiggled her fingers until he pulled her to standing. Her shorts were very short, and she had the longest legs I'd ever seen on a girl, like a loping giraffe. The dry grass left imprints across the backs of her thighs like pound signs.

The youngest sister, Phoebe, abandoned her towel and crawled toward me on all fours like a bad dog.

"Drew, Drew, Drew," she cooed. "You don't remember me, do you?"

I made a face. Um, no, I didn't. As far as I knew, we'd never met, and if we had, I prayed for those memories to stay erased.

Phoebe laughed. An ugly sound. In fact, she was kind of an ugly girl. Too-white skin, too-skinny body, with scabs all over her arms and legs. Bug bites, I guessed, but it looked like she was falling apart. Her hair glinted red like Charlie's but held none of the prettiness. Plus, she wore it pulled back in a ponytail, and a big chunk was missing from the left side. She caught me gawking.

"I fell asleep with gum in my mouth," she explained.

"Oh."

"You like to swim?" She had a yellow suit on beneath a pair of cutoff overalls.

"Sure."

"We can go to Walden Pond if you want. Tons of kids go there." She made a vague gesture in what I thought was a southward direction.

"Okay," I said. A pond? Actually I'd never been in anything but a pool. The idea of not knowing how deep the water was unsettled me. But a pond? It couldn't be that big, could it?

"My dad can bring his canoe out," Phoebe said.

I frowned. All I knew about my uncle Kirby, I'd picked up from my grandmother. Apparently, he was a disappointment.

"I don't like boats," I told Phoebe.

"Why not?"

My face burned. Boats were like cars. Intolerable. "I don't want to talk about it."

"What grade are you in?" she asked.

"Fifth."

"I'm going to the middle school next year. I can't wait."

"Oh," I said, because I couldn't think of anything else to say.

She shrugged, leaned over, and whispered in my ear, "Do you know why you're here?" The sickly sweet wafts of her grape soda filled my nostrils.

"Where?"

"Here. This summer. In Concord. You've never come before. Only Keith."

"My parents made me come."

Her jaw dropped. "You mean you didn't want to?"

"No. I want to go home!"

"What? We're not good enough for you?"

The oldest sister, Anna, who'd said nothing so far, interjected at this point, "Phoebe, don't."

"Don't what?"

"Don't tease him. He's . . ." Anna ran her eyes over me. She was sixteen, practically a grown-up, with long dark hair and very fine features, like one of Siobhan's handmade dolls. Anna had authority. In her voice, in the easy way she moved. I stared at her eagerly. I was what?

"He's not happy," she finished.

chapter
thirteen

matter

I see Jordan again. Late Friday night. Standing by the covered bridge.

The moon is out, very full, and it's easy to recognize her short hair and folded arms. But Jordan doesn't see me. I make sure of that. I cling to the shadows pooling beneath the trees with my heart pounding and my blood pumping.

All of my senses are alive.

I glance skyward. I tell myself to be careful, but I'm lonely. That makes all the difference in the world. It's not my normal loneliness, either, the kind where I put up all sorts of walls, like cruelty and arrogance and silence. This is a childish ache, a primitive need to be reminded I exist. I don't like it, but what can I do? I'm human. Sort of. Enough. And hell, I'm a guy. If I don't take care of certain needs on a regular basis, then these kinds of thoughts are unavoidable.

That's evolution for you.

The whisper of my feet cutting through the long grass is drowned out by the drone of the current. Jordan doesn't hear my approach. I am stealthy. I think she's scared to cross the river, and I don't blame her. It's close to midnight. Who knows what's out there?

"Hey," I say softly.

She gasps and whirls around. Jordan's on the trail and I'm still down in the meadow, so for once she doesn't have to break her neck looking up at me. We're eye to eye.

Her shoulders relax. "Hey, Win."

"What are you doing?"

She jerks her head toward the mountain. "I'm trying to get to Eden, but I forgot a flashlight."

"Oh." So she intends to go to the party. Friday nights in Eden are a tradition around here. Students sneak out and gather in this secret spot every week so long as the weather's decent. From what I can tell, this has been going on for generations. For three years running, on alumni weekend, I've been approached by hordes of gray-haired, grim-faced former students, and they all have the same question for me. They don't ask about new classes or old teachers or what college I hope to attend. Instead they lower their voices, fill their eyes with reverence, and point across the river, deep into the woods, while asking, "Do you still go? Do you still go to Paradise?"

Their Paradise of yesterday is what we call Eden today. And I know how badly they want my answer to be yes, so that's what I say, but in truth I don't go.

Not to party, anyway.

I glance at Jordan. "You don't need a flashlight. The moon's bright enough."

"Really?"

"Really. But aren't the woods off-limits?"

"They are," she says. "That's not stopping anybody, though."

"You sure about that?"

Jordan sighs and fiddles with the collar of her shirt, something striped with buttons. We're actually dressed pretty similarly, now that I think about it. The only difference is she's got motorcycle boots on, soft black leather, and here I am, slogging around in a pair of old Sauconys.

Her hips shift. "Sure, I'm sure. Come on, Win. Just lead the way, okay?"

"Wait. Did you think I was going up there?"

"You aren't?"

"No."

Her dark eyes widen. "Then why are you out here?"

I'm trying to reach the stars.

Now that's a good question, but I can't tell her the answer. If I do, I'm screwed. Plus she looks distressed. I doubt she'll ask for my help again, which I admire, but the thought of her hiking in the dark by herself, ending up with all those drunk assholes who will just try and—

"I'll take you," I say before I know what I'm doing, and I regret the words the moment they leave my mouth.

But it's already too late to take them back.

Jordan nods gratefully, so we head off. Together, we cross the covered bridge and enter the woods, following a well-worn path that takes us straight up the mountainside.

Almost immediately, the night comes alive. Everywhere, in all directions, there's sound and there's movement—swooping bats and screeching owls and rustling shadows. As we climb higher, a yawning ravine tumbles down into pure black nothingness and only slants of moonlight pinpricking through the tree branches light the way before us.

The path narrows. We're forced to walk single file.

Soon it feels like we've been out here forever. If I didn't know better, I'd say hours or days, but the truth would be counted in minutes. Time behaves differently in the wild, I think. Space, too—all of it stretching, evolving into something new, something unheard of. And the farther we get from school, the riper the air swells with a danger I cannot see.

Only feel.

My pulse picks up, a heady rush of despair.

This was not a good idea.

But our feet keep moving.

I keep us moving, because I can't stop and think about how I shouldn't be doing this. How Jordan shouldn't be out here in the first place. Not alone and not with me. But I can't change my mind. We're nearly there.

So I lead.

And she follows.

Up, up, up.

I am like Orpheus returning Eurydice from the underworld.

Except I never once look back.

We make it. The distant glow of fire-flame leaping and licking up the rocky wall of the hollow signals our arrival, and the dirt trail we're on dips down into the remote valley that opens onto Eden.

Jordan gasps. She's never seen the mountain clearing at night. The drama is undeniable. White-green grass sways in the moon glow and music fills the air, something angry, fever-pitched. Students throng near the base of the rock hollow, spread around a massive bonfire, all dancing, touching, flirting, groping. A makeshift bar's been set up on a level patch of ground, and nearby, a raucous crowd plays strip poker beneath a flaming row of tiki torches. There are even a couple of tents set up in the distance, on the meadow's far side, but I definitely don't want to know what's going on in those.

In fact, I don't want to be here at all.

I turn to go, to slink back into the night where I belong, but something clamps around my wrist. I nearly leap out of my skin but manage to keep my reflexes in check. When I glance down, I see Jordan's hand. She's holding on to me for dear life.

"Thanks for walking me up here," she whispers. The breeze catches her short bangs and her face scrunches up. She's got the scowl of a razorbill.

The sooner you let go, the sooner I can leave.

I'm about half a second away from wrenching my arm free when a flashlight beam cuts across my face, blinding me. I throw my other arm up. I can't see who's approaching, but then I hear the jeering laughter and it's so obvious.

Lex.

Something dark scrabbles through my chest. I want to grab him, shake him, but I don't trust my instincts, so I just watch as he takes a long slug of something from a paper bag and lurches straight for Jordan. He pulls her from me, out into the moonlit clearing, but I don't feel any sense of relief, because now he's got his hands all over her waist, her ass, and he's sticking his tongue down her throat.

My ears roar. A rush of blood. I feel woozy. Is this how it begins? I want to listen to my body, but my mind won't shut up. Does she like it? I don't know, but I don't think so, not by the way she writhes free and shoves Lex in the chest so hard that his flashlight falls to the ground. But then she's laughing and he's laughing, too, only her hands shake like autumn leaves and she's not making eye contact with him. Or me.

Lex continues to drink from his stupid paper bag. "Our junior transfer," he slurs. "I'm so glad you made it. Best thing in life, new girls. God bless 'em. But tell me your name again. It's . . . it's . . ."

"Jordan," she says firmly. "Herrera."

"Jordan. Lovely Jordan." Lex swivels in my direction, legs unsteady. I haven't moved. I'm still hidden in shadows. "And who's this? Don't tell me you've brought a date."

"Don't tell me it's any of your business," Jordan says, and Lex's laugh is like a foghorn. He leans down to nuzzle her again, but Jordan does this deft ducking maneuver and his ass nearly ends up on the ground.

The laugh grows louder. "Never mind, love. Cute as you are in your androgynous sort of way, you certainly aren't any fun. I almost feel sorry for your guy."

Jordan's hands go to her hips. "That's fine. Win and I are just friends anyway."

We are?

"Hold up. Did you say *Win*?" All of a sudden Lex is bent over, scrambling to retrieve his flashlight. He grabs it. He shines it directly in my eyes.

"Oh, shit," he breathes. "It *is* you. What're you doing here?"

I glower.

Lex pushes hair off his forehead. "You and I, we need to talk."

"Leave him alone," Jordan snaps. She's caught sight of the expression on my face.

"Win," Lex says, pleading. "I'm serious."

"I'm serious about leaving him alone." Jordan positions herself right beneath Lex's nose, so he's forced to look at her. "You're crazy if you think Win wants to talk to you."

Lex laughs again, only it's a different sound this time, almost sad, almost pained. "No, *he's* the crazy one, love. Like a danger to himself and others. Haven't you figured that out yet? This guy needs some serious—"

I lunge for him. I don't realize I'm doing it until Jordan steps between us. She grabs on to me, drags me back by the elbow.

"Knock it off," she growls.

"How's your tennis game, Win?" Lex calls out, but Jordan flips him off as she marches away, still pulling me with her.

We end up in front of the bar area, which consists of a cooler full of cheap beer and a sticky card table scattered with half-empty bottles of the worst kind of liquor. Sour Apple Pucker. Southern Comfort. That rum that smells like coconuts.

Jordan digs around for two bottles of Coors and offers one to me. My decision's a no-brainer. If I drink, I'll just have to puke it up later since alcohol absolutely does not fall within my daily allotted calories and there's no way I'm fucking up my shot at the state title this year. Despite my God-given talent for endurance, long-distance running hasn't been my primary sport before now, and I need something good in my life. Something I've earned. I shake my head at Jordan. Her lips purse, but she puts the bottle back and twists open her own.

She's embarrassed for me. We both are. I can tell.

"So, team captain," she says after a moment, "got any words of inspiration for me tonight?"

Startled, I look right at her. The roaring in my ears quiets. Her chin's held up, still tough, and her lips are pulled back in a wry smile. Jordan's teasing, but she's also offering something. What, I don't know, but it brings out my own smile, tentative, but far less awkward than usual.

"Absolutely none," I say.

Her smile grows wider and less wry.

"You want to sit?" She points, and I shouldn't. I should go. I should be alone. I should stop thinking and just *be*.

But I'm doing it.

I'm following her toward the bonfire.

I'm sitting beside her on a smooth, wide rock.

Jordan's got her motorcycle boots tucked beneath her butt and I've got my feet flat on the ground and I'm trying not to let my leg touch hers because that would be weird. It's also a challenge, seeing as we're squeezed so close together, right between these tight clusters of students who haven't given us a second look because we're nobody and they don't want to share their weed. Thank God.

"You don't drink?" she asks.

"Not if I can help it."

"Meaning there are times you can't?"

"You'd be surprised," I say, and she sort of smirks, but in a way that makes me think she's confused. That's good. It's a sign I'm in control again.

"God, that Lex guy was such an ass," she says. "I'm so sorry."

Well, in truth, *she's* part of the reason he was such an ass just now. I know that. I once fooled around with a girl Lex liked and he's never forgiven me. But I'm not explaining all that to Jordan, and besides, the fact Lex wants to talk to me is what's really out of the range of ordinary.

I don't like it.

Not tonight.

I glance at Jordan. "Don't worry about it."

She sighs. "Well, I'm also sorry I made you come all this way."

"It's fine."

"Wow, Win. I almost believe you when you say that."

I respond to her sarcasm with a listless roll of my shoulders.

"You got low self-esteem or something?" she asks.

"What are you talking about?"

"I just mean, you let that guy crap all over you—tonight, the other day by the river. And if you actually—"

"Jordan, don't," I say.

"Don't what?"

"Don't think you know me."

"I don't think that! It's just, I'm *trying* to get to know you. And I'm not being judgmental, I swear. Lord knows I'm not in a position to judge anyone—"

"Oh, yeah? Why's that?"

She grimaces, pointing to her beer before taking another swig. It's already two-thirds empty. "Let's change the subject, okay?"

"Are you asking my *permission*?"

"So," Jordan says, her voice rising in pitch and decibels, "I didn't know you played tennis."

The crawling on my skin is like that involuntary response you get when coming across a pile of maggots or a nest of hatching spiders. Purely visceral. Like my body just wants to give up and die.

"I don't play anymore," I tell her through clenched teeth. "Never again."

chapter
fourteen

antimatter

Simplify, simplify.

Later, the five of us found bikes in our grandfather's shed and rode out to Walden Pond. I pedaled as fast as I could to outrun the deerflies, but once there, I just stood, frozen, on the shore in my swim trunks. Kids screamed and splashed all around me. Apparently ponds *could* be big. Like really big. I frowned. Technically, this was a lake. I was sure of it.

My toes curled around the pebbles that lined the beach. Maybe I shouldn't go in. There were no lifeguards anywhere, just a couple of adults sitting at picnic tables, looking at their phones.

A yellow blur whizzed past me, launching into the water like a rocket. Then it called my name.

Phoebe.

I took a step closer.

"What are you doing?" she shouted. "Are your legs broken?"

"I don't know if I feel like swimming," I called back.

"But you're the one who asked to come here!"

No, I hadn't.

"Come on!" Phoebe waved her hands so wildly, it looked like she was having a seizure. The bald spot on the side of her head glistened with water and sun. I hurried toward her just to make her stop.

She grinned and splashed water on the crotch of my trunks as I waded in, which made me mad. Then she turned and swam away. Afraid of what people would think if I didn't, I followed her out to the raft, where I sat while the other kids jostled me, taking turns doing cannonballs and baby spankers. My head began to throb. Too much sun. Too much motion. I didn't see Keith anywhere, but when I asked Phoebe, she pointed, and I spied him and Charlie on the other side of the pond. They sat together on a boulder half-submerged in water. Their knees were touching. My head kept throbbing.

Two hours of swimming did nothing to reduce the humidity. Or bugs. On our way back from the pond we stopped for ice cream in an area the girls referred to as "uptown Concord." The place itself was called Winston's. We didn't go inside, just ordered from the sidewalk at the walk-up window. I wanted a plain strawberry cone, but Phoebe insisted I get it with something called "jimmies." A Boston thing, apparently. My southern instincts told me there were probably racial undertones to the term, but I ordered them anyway. Jimmies turned out to be chocolate sprinkles. They looked like ants and fell all over my shirt when I tried to lick the ice cream. Phoebe and Charlie laughed, but Keith made me the maddest. He kept calling *me* Winston, which was my middle name, and I didn't like it.

"Stop saying that," I told him.

"Why? It's a stuck-up name for a stuck-up kid."

I didn't understand where this was coming from. "I'm not stuck-up!"

Keith sneered. "Oh yes you are, dear *Winston*. The little tennis star. Mr. Four Point Five. Do you know how much it's costing Mom and Dad to send you to that fancy club?"

Now Anna laughed, too. I felt my cheeks redden and stalked off a few storefronts down Thoreau Street, where I dumped my ice cream into a garbage can. Then I kicked the curb so hard it felt like I'd broken half the bones in my foot. My chest heaved and my eyes stung. I didn't understand how Keith could be so mean. He knew how homesick I was. This was definitely Charlie's fault, it had to be, with her snotty attitude and those stupid long animal legs. I hated her.

Phoebe joined me. We stood next to each other on the street, facing traffic. I wouldn't look at her. Wouldn't talk. Wished she'd just go away. The butt of her shorts was all wet from her swimsuit underneath. So embarrassing.

"Come on," she said finally, her lips ringed with so many jimmies it looked like she had bugs crawling out of her mouth. "We're leaving."

chapter
fifteen

matter

"So do you like girls or what?"

Jordan doesn't answer me right away. Instead she fingers away the label on her second beer and watches the fire. She's been doing that for a while now, the fire watching, and I don't get what's so interesting. We're not close enough to see the creeping embers, and someone just threw a new log on, so there's all this smoke and ash. But maybe it's more exciting than looking at me.

"Why are you asking me that?" she says finally.

"I was just wondering."

"From what I know about you, Win, that seems very out of character. Wondering. But whatever."

"Yeah, well, you didn't seem to like it when Lex kissed you earlier."

Jordan lets out a laugh. It's a loud one, like she's buzzed already or might think I'm slow. "So *that* makes me a lesbian? Okay. Sure. Fine. Because there couldn't be any other possible reason why I wouldn't like Lex kissing me."

I focus on keeping my nerves steady, but a shudder of wrath works its way through my bones.

"I'm sorry," I say. "I shouldn't have let him do that."

She shrugs. "He's just drunk."

"That's no excuse."

"Except when it is." Jordan tips her bottle in my direction.

I watch her drink. More.

She side-eyes me back.

"What?" she asks.

"Why were you looking at me in the chapel the other day?"

She puts her bottle down. "Is *that* why you want to know who I like? To find out if I like *you*?"

I say nothing.

Jordan's head bobs. "Hey, maybe you're not as different as I thought you were."

"Different than who?"

"Everyone."

"What does that mean?"

"Well, just, sometimes you're kind of weird, you know?"

"Mmm." Yeah, I know. Trust me.

She leans back, elbows on rock. "Let me guess, Win. When you run out of better options tonight, you gonna try and get me naked?"

"No," I say. "I'm not."

This gets Jordan's head to turn. The weight of her gaze is intense, but when I'm honest, I'm honest. I always stand by my words.

I don't look away.

After a moment, she grins.

"So tell me," she says, as her eyes do this twinkling thing, "do you like girls or what?"

A surprise: I laugh with her. Mirth rumbles my body like an earthquake. I'm rusty, but it feels good. And yes, I say, I do like girls. I don't pursue them, though, and there are a lot of reasons for that. It's gotten me in trouble before, but I also think I have ridiculously high standards because the whole dating, fooling around thing seems so complicated. And not in a good way. I hate obligations, and if you want to be with a girl, it's like you're expected to *do* certain things. And do them in a certain way. Sit with her at meals. Ask about her day. Not talk to people she doesn't like. Someone should write a book about what a guy's supposed to do because it's confusing as hell. And from what I can tell, it's not worth it. Unless . . . unless the girl is absolutely perfect.

Or unless you just can't help yourself.

Case in point, the time Lex pushed me into dating at the start of our sophomore year. I only went along with it because he insisted and because he was always bragging like he was so experienced. Like he knew better than me. I mean, the way he tells it, he's like a certified expert on dating and attraction, but I've never bought into it. There's a waft of desperation in the way he goes after girls, in his compulsive need to plan things perfectly so they can't back out. Still, the one he set me up with was decent enough. She was his girl's best friend and a balle-rina, and I did everything he told me to. Then one night after study hours he brought her to our room and left us alone, and it was like she was waiting for me to do stuff to her. I could tell by the way she got quiet and put her hand on the front of my pants and made all these breathy sounds so that her nonexis-tent chest moved up and down. Nothing about that was appealing, but after a few more get-togethers, *she* ended up kissing me. And I can't lie, that was kind of exciting, but I couldn't stop thinking about what she was thinking. Or why she wanted my tongue in her mouth. Or what she'd want me to do next. Lex told me to try going further, but he didn't tell me *how*. And what was the point of it all? I just got so uncomfortable after kissing her that I ended up doing what I already did by myself anyway. And the ballerina wasn't the one I thought of when I did *that*.

"Then who was?" Jordan asks.

"Who was what?"

"You know, who did you think about when you were fourteen and jacking off?"

I straighten up. "You're blunt, aren't you?"

"No. You're coy. There's a difference."

"I see. And I was fifteen, by the way."

She's not listening. "But you're not shy. You didn't care that I saw you with your pants down the other day. And now you're telling me about your sexual failures."

"I never said I was shy."

"But you're not denying the failure part."

Damn, she's sharp. But really, "sexual failure" sounds more lurid than the truth. Like I need Cialis or a blueprint to the female body or something. But it wasn't like that. The ballerina and I kissed one last time and she tried pulling my shirt up, getting me to do the same to her, and I didn't want to. By that point I'd already noticed things about her that I didn't like. Like the way she always wanted me to talk about "my feelings" and then got mad when I had the wrong ones. And she definitely wasn't as pretty as I'd originally thought. Up close she had bad skin and dark roots, and I always got a good view of the hairs living inside her nostrils when we were kissing. Not exactly a turn-on. But the awkwardness carried over to our next date: a trip to Manchester with Lex and his girl to see some band they all liked and that I didn't know. We rode down in a van with some other students, and I forgot my pressure-point wristbands and the motion sickness was awful. Not puking-all-over-the-place awful, but pretty close, and my head hurt so bad, I couldn't talk. Not even when we got to the show, which was in the basement of some grungy coffee shop right off Main Street, and everyone there just spent the whole time name-dropping and showing off their band swag and indie persuasions. The ballerina assumed I didn't like her, and well, she lost interest. Drifted off. Said some things to some people.

It's for the best, really.

"I'm not denying anything," I say.

Jordan nudges me. "You have your secrets, though. They must be dark ones if you'll talk about this kind of stuff so casually."

"I guess."

"What did Lex mean when he said you were crazy?"

"Ask him."

"I don't want to."

I stretch my shoulders. I have to say something. "For a while, when I got angry, I used to hurt myself, okay? Punch walls. Punch myself. I don't know why. I did other things, too. It was beyond stupid."

Her mouth falls open. "You did? Seriously?"

"Yeah."

"And now?"

"Now I don't get angry."

She mulls this over. "You're still hiding something."

My gaze drifts to the moon. "Yeah, probably."

"I'm sorry," she says. "I shouldn't be so pushy."

The silence that follows is comfortable. My chest opens. It's like I can breathe again. We've left the topic of Lex and secrets.

Jordan speaks first. "Hey, Win?"

"Yeah."

"Can we talk about girls again? I bet I can figure out your type. I'm good at that."

Uh-oh. My type? "Sure."

She cocks her head while she inspects me, her brown eyes running all the way from tip to tail. "You're tall. Like six feet, right?"

I nod.

"Hmm. Putting that together with the whole tennis and running thing, I'm guessing you go for sporty over that ballerina. Anna Kournikova? Is that the girl of your dreams?"

"Not even close," I say, but a familiar shiver racks my spine. Titillating and guilt-laced.

Wrong girl. Right name.

chapter sixteen

antimatter

I cried out when Keith grabbed my arm.

"What's wrong with you?" he snapped, leaning over the bed where I lay. "Charlie's waiting. Get up."

He'd already gotten dressed and had breakfast. Me, I'd missed practice. I hadn't been able to move that far.

Specks of July haze filtered in through the lace curtains, the day already overtired and overhot. I hated the impatience in his tone. I strained to push off the mattress, but the sharp pain in my abdomen made me whimper. I twisted my head toward the wall.

Keith's voice lowered. "Come on, Drew. You're okay."

"No, I'm not!"

"What? You're really sick or something?"

I pressed my head against the scratchy pillowcase and nodded.

"You need me to get Gram?" he asked.

No, I didn't need that. Not at all. Our grandmother hadn't
warmed up to me since that first night. I said all the wrong
things around her and she thought I was dumb. I knew she did.
Keith, on the other hand, was loved, doted on. She'd even taken
him into Cambridge to some famous bookstore, and when she
went grocery shopping, she bought him vegetarian bacon,
which tasted awful just like I knew it would. All I got were the
dirty looks and chilly admonishments to stay quiet, act my age,
and mind my manners. But I couldn't help myself. I mewled
again, a tortured sound. Keith scooted from the room to get her.

Two minutes later brought a flurry of footsteps and whispering in the hallway.

"What's wrong with him?" And there it was. My grandmother's voice, dripping with scorn.

"I think it's his stomach. He hasn't . . . I don't think he's gone
to the bathroom since he got here."

"He hasn't gone in *six days*?"

The hallway rang with a bevy of giggles. God, was that
Charlie out there? And *Phoebe*?

I withered beneath the blankets. Wished death on the entire
world.

Keith cleared his throat. "Well, maybe, I think, maybe he
should see a doctor. He's crying."

"He doesn't need a doctor," my grandmother said firmly. "I'll
be right back."

There was more giggling in the hall and then a knock on the
door.

"Go away!" I shouted. The last thing I wanted was for everyone to crowd around and laugh more. Why would they do that? Why? It wasn't funny. It *hurt*.

"It's just me, Drew," came a soft voice.

My stomach flipped over in a way that had nothing to do with my digestive issues. It was Anna, the elder cousin. She slid through a crack in the door and sat beside me. Her pale green dress was the same color as the leaves on the willow branches outside. I breathed her in, with my nose, my eyes, my everything— that long dark hair, that earthy warmth that smelled like digging flower beds in the spring with Siobhan, that syrupy way she melted into the blankets. My heart rate slowed. Suddenly I didn't care that I had nothing on but a pair of pajama pants. I just wanted to crawl into her lap and stay there.

She rubbed my back. "I'm sorry you don't feel good."

I curled closer.

My grandmother swooped in then. "Sit up, Andrew."

I wouldn't let any moans of pain escape me, not in Anna's presence. I was brave. I propped myself into sitting and ignored the fire raging in my midsection. Let my skinny legs dangle over the side of the bed. My grandmother jabbed at my gut with dry hands. I stiffened and resisted the urge to bite her.

"Does anything else hurt?" she asked.

I shook my head.

"This wouldn't happen if you ate the food I made instead of sneaking downstairs at night and gorging yourself on junk."

Oh, great. She knew. I looked away.

Smack! Her hand came out too quickly for me to register, ringing me with a sharp slap across the face.

"Pay attention when I talk to you!"

My lip curled. I wasn't scared. Or hurt. Something awful came alive inside of me. A million images rushed into my head. Images of bad things. Very bad things. Things I could do.

"I'll give him that, Gram," Anna said quickly, taking the spoon and jar of medicine out of her hand. "He's just embarrassed to have us all looking at him."

"Mmm."

After she'd left, Anna touched my face but said nothing.

"She's so mean!"

"Don't hold it against her," Anna said.

"Well, I don't like her. I don't have to like her!"

"No, you don't. But you do have to listen to her."

I pouted. "Why? She hates me. And she loves everyone else."

"She loves us all."

"Then why doesn't she act like it?"

"Because love doesn't always look nice."

I folded my arms even tighter. Did Anna think I deserved to be slapped? Because I was bad? That's what it sounded like. My chest swelled with bubbles of shame. Maybe I *was* bad. All those mean thoughts in my mind, wanting to hurt people. My grandmother knew about Soren, maybe she knew other things. The kinds of pictures I liked to look at on the computer. The kinds of things I liked to read.

"Take this." Anna waved a spoonful of frothy liquid before me.

I twisted my head. "It looks gross."

"It's milk of magnesia. And you definitely want to take it because if you don't, Gram'll come back in here and do something worse."

"Like what?"

Anna grinned wide, the happiest I'd seen her. She rubbed her nose against mine. Eskimo kissing, we called it at school, but I never let anyone do it to me because I hated being touched. But Anna was different. Her skin was very soft, like the velvety folds of Pilot's ears. The shame bubbles popped and my heart went all tingly. Anna was better than my mom. Maybe I loved her.

"I don't know," she said teasingly. "She might give you an enema or something. Wouldn't that be awful?"

The tingling stopped and black dots danced in front of my eyes. I definitely did not want that. I opened my mouth wide. Anna stuck the spoon in.

Later, when I felt better and lighter, a thunderstorm washed across the state. Heavy drops of rain pummeled the earth like sniper fire and the air smelled bright and raw like ozone. I stood at the window and watched one of my grandfather's spit cans roll off a pine bench and straight into the back pond, where it bobbed around before sinking. My grandmother's herb garden was completely underwater. Half the plants had been washed away or flattened. I smiled.

Light footsteps approached. I dove back under the covers as Anna popped her head in again. She'd called in sick to her job at the local library so that she could take care of me.

"Still not feeling well?" she asked.

I pressed my cheek against the pillow and made sad eyes.

She sat beside me, soft thighs touching my knees. The fear-anger-confusion that lived inside me subsided, like the lowering tide.

Anna rubbed my back again.

I felt happy.

chapter

seventeen

matter

"You can go if you want," Jordan tells me. "I don't need a baby-sitter."

My heart skips a beat, not in a lovey-dovey way, please, but in a *holy shit, ladies and gentlemen, mark the date and time, Winston Winters is being pushed away before he can withdraw sulkily* kind of way. I feel a little sick, actually. How did this happen? I'm not dense. Being pushed away implies I'm making an effort to stick around.

Something is very wrong.

I take a steadying breath and pull out my phone. A quick check confirms what I already know, what I can already sense — it's late.

Later than it should be.

The sick feeling intensifies. I'm too keyed up. Anxious, maybe, I guess. Although "anxiety" is one of those words people at our boarding school throw around that's hard for me to connect with. Kind of goes hand in hand with that whole "worry" thing. I don't get that, either. Why get worked up over the bad thing that hasn't happened yet when there're plenty of bad things that have?

Take Teddy, for example. He's a day student, but he and Lex have been tight since the first day of school, so I know him pretty well. The guy worries about everything. It's draining to see. Never mind that his family is beyond nuclear-ideal—I stay with his folks during vacations or whenever I can get away with not going back to Virginia—he's loaded, drives a 3 Series BMW, gets perfect grades, and even if he didn't, what would it matter? Teddy's a three-generation legacy at Brown, and really, if grades were going to make or break his college success, he'd be better off at public school, where his über-achievement and 4.3 GPA might actually impress somebody. He can't see that, though. Instead, the guy's on every SSRI in the book, pops Ambien just to sleep, and practically faints anytime a girl says hi to him. At sixteen. It's ridiculous. Literally nothing bad has ever happened to him. He just *thinks* it will. As if thinking will help.

Thinking never helps. I know that.

"Teddy," I asked him once, back when I still thought it was important to try to fit in, "will you feel less bad when a girl rejects you if you worry about it ahead of time?"

"Screw you," he sniped. "So you're saying she's going to reject me no matter what?"

"That's not what I said at all."

He sniffed. "Well, if I worry about it, odds are I won't ask her out in the first place. And I'll still hate myself. Happy?"

I clenched my jaw. "Never."

Teddy shook a finger at me. "No way, Winters. I get to be miserable, too. You don't get to be the best at everything."

But tonight, anxiety makes sense. Intellectually, I *should* be nervous. But do I feel it? Is that the reason I'm still sitting next to a girl I don't know, running at the mouth about my *personal life*? Of all things.

The moon peeks at me from behind a stormy cloud.

It's full. Alluring.

My tongue runs along the tips of my teeth.

It's an old, old habit.

Jordan slouches over on my right. She thinks I'm ignoring her. This can't be how she wanted to spend the evening. This can't be why she came. I mean, I know what she wants. She wants to meet people. Make friends. Be normal. And to do that, she needs me to get up. To tell her I don't need her to babysit me, either.

I can do that.

I will do that.

I get to my feet. "See you around, Jordan."

"Sure thing," she says. Her fingers work to spike her short boy hair so that it stands straight up and down. I don't think she's aware she's doing it, which is kind of endearing, but it also sort of hurts to watch.

"Don't walk back through the woods by yourself," I tell her. "I'm serious. Ask Teddy if you can't find somebody. He's over there playing cards. He's got glasses and a black shirt that says 'Burn Hollywood Burn.'"

This startles her. She looks like she wants to ask why I'm so concerned, then seems to think better of it. Perhaps she remembers the details about the townie's death and the words the news stations used to describe his killing: "torn apart." "Eviscerated." And my personal favorite: "partially consumed."

She gives me a nod and a weak smile. "Thanks again, Win. I really liked talking with you. Let's do it again sometime."

I blink. "Just remember what I said."

Then I turn on my heel and walk away.

Swiftly.

chapter

eighteen

antimatter

"Don't you dare get on any rides, Drew! I swear to God, if you puke on yourself, I'll wring your goddamn neck." Keith towered Eiffel-tall, backing me against a cotton candy cart. I trembled. This was not my Keith. This Keith had narrow eyes and smelled of hair gel and aftershave. This Keith looked older. Meaner. Wildly unfamiliar.

"I'm not getting on any rides!" I snapped, although I kind of wanted to, just to spite him. Maybe I'd fall out.

"Here, just take this already." He shoved a handful of bills in my face, then turned and loped over to where Charlie stood waiting in line for the Ferris wheel.

I jammed the cash into the front pocket of my cargo shorts

and stalked down the carnival midway, my vision blurred with rage. I had no idea where I was going, but it was Fourth of July weekend and the place was beginning to fill up.

Dusk hovered on the edge of night, but that did nothing to thwart the New England mugginess. As I wound through the crowd, a watery heat clung to me, filling every pore, every fold, every touch of skin to skin. The heavy weight of summer.

The sharp scent of popcorn, sugar, and deep-frying oil made my mouth water as I lurched past the food stands, but I kept walking. I didn't stop. I didn't want to eat alone. Keith might be eager to ditch me, but I knew Phoebe would let me tag along with her and her friends. Or she would if I could just find her. My shoes kicked up fairground dust as I trudged around and around the maze of rides and games. This was useless. I couldn't even text her because she'd managed to ruin her third phone in a year by dropping it in the toilet. Her dad had been seriously mad. Phoebe didn't seem to care.

"Probably for the best," she told me. "Those things give you titty cancer anyway."

I wasn't a hundred percent sure, but from what I could tell, Phoebe did not have titties.

"I think you mean brain cancer," I said.

Eye roll. "Whatever."

I picked up pace as I passed the Orbitron, one of those massive octopus-armed rides. Only this one didn't just whip around at breakneck speed, the arms actually moved up and down in the air while spinning. Forget puking, I'd probably stroke out if I got on that thing. After that came a cluster of kiddie rides, including one consisting of these alarmingly painted "bumblebees" that should have been shut down for aesthetic reasons, if not racially offensive ones. I paused. Scanned the crowd again.

"Hey, kid." A gruff voice reached me, stretching from the shadows beneath the bleachers of the pig-racing track.

I ignored it.

"Get over here, kid. You too good to answer me when I talk to you?"

I finally turned around. It was a game operator doing the talking, and he was just as scary as I thought he'd be. Fat. Greasy. Bearded. His hands hidden beneath a striped apron. I drew myself up as tall as I could. Made a mean face.

He roared. A phlegmy sound. "Damn, kid. Who shit on your parade?"

I cracked a smile.

"That's better. Now get over here," he repeated. "Easy win."

"N-no, thanks."

He hawked, then spit. "I'll make you a deal. How 'bout that? Five balls, five dollars. Best price of the night. Guaranteed winner." He gave a tip of his head to the row of hanging Sponge-Bob dolls. It looked like some reenactment of a mass lynching.

I swallowed. I didn't want to play. At all. But it'd be rude to ignore his offer, wouldn't it? I walked over and pulled a twenty out of my pocket. My legs weakened when his callused fingers touched mine. The twenty disappeared beneath the apron. A ten came back in its place. I stared. Took the bill without comment.

The guy stepped back and gestured to the row of basketballs. "It's all yours, kid. Show me what you got."

The first ball nearly slipped from my grasp, my hands were so slick with sweat. The shot bounced off the rim and rolled toward a hay bale. The carny yawned and pulled out a cigarette. Lit up and turned his attention to his phone.

Pull it together, Drew. You don't lose. Ever.

I shuddered back in time. Not to the moment when Soren Nichols raised his arms in victory, but to the exact moment when I hit him. I hadn't forgotten the feel of bone breaking beneath skin. The thrill. I took a deep breath and held the second ball between both hands. Went through the same routine I used before I made my serve in tennis. I squared my feet and visualized the ball leaving my hands and swishing straight through the net. Then I let my mind whisper one word:

Perfect.

I bent my legs and took the shot without a doubt in my mind. Pure beauty. The ball went right in. I tossed my head and looked at the carny.

"Hey," I said. "I won."

Twin streams of smoke puffed from his nostrils like dragon's breath. He didn't take his eyes off the phone. "Didn't see it," he said. "I gotta see the shot for it to count."

"No way. That . . . that went in!"

He gave a disinterested shrug. "Try again."

My voice lowered. "I want my money back."

"And I want your mom to keep me warm at night. Fuck off, kid. Your whining's starting to piss me off."

I whirled back around, snatched up the third ball, wheeled, and pitched it as hard as I could. Another perfect shot. It slammed off the back of his head. The phone clattered to the ground.

He moved with superhuman speed, sidewinding toward me with his ugly face twisted in rage. Even with my knees knocking, I stayed right where I was. I wouldn't run. I just wouldn't. Not even when I saw his right hand come out from beneath the apron with something bright and glinting. *A knife,* my mind whispered. *He's got a knife.*

I still didn't run.

Get over here, kid.

I clenched my fists.

I want your mom to keep me warm at night.

I took a step toward him.

"Drew! Dreeeeeeeeeew!" Phoebe's annoying squawk cut the

standoff. She swooped down on me, grabbing my hand and tugging. A crowd of kids swarmed behind her. She glanced at the carny, who'd frozen in his tracks, then she looked away. She didn't give him a moment's thought. I stared at his hands. There was no knife. I blinked and shook my head, confused.

I let Phoebe pull me along. I didn't look back.

"I've been searching all over for you!" she cried. "The pig races start in like five minutes!"

"I couldn't find you, either," I said.

She flipped her braids over her shoulder. "That's because you're over here playing *games*. God, you're so clueless. It's like you're blond or something. Come on, we have to push if we want to get right up front."

Push? That's when I saw the thick mass of people clumping to get into the arena, cattle-drive crazy. Painted pictures of the racers stampeded above their heads. *Pork 'n' Rec. Hogwarts X-press. Jessica Squeal. Snoop Hoggy Hog.*

I stopped short. Nerves caught up with me. My stomach tossed and rolled like a bottle in the surf.

Phoebe spun around. Gave me a *what now?* look.

"I don't want to go in," I said.

She groaned. "Are. You. Kidding. Me. I've been waiting all night to see this."

"Well, you go on, then. I said I don't want to!"

"Fine! You're beyond stupid. I hope you know that." She jabbed me in the chest with her finger. "Find me later. I'm not waiting for you."

I turned and walked off.

My mind crackled. My skin felt electric.

Sssnap!

Get over here, Drew.

I left the fairgrounds and headed out toward the dirt parking lot, veering neatly around an endless line of Porta-Potties.

My breath came in short, choppy bursts. The bad images were back. The really bad ones. They colonized my head and multiplied. I wanted them to go, to leave me alone, but more than anything I longed to douse that carny with gasoline, light him on fire, and watch him burn.

I entered the parking lot and kept walking. I reached down and picked a large jagged rock off the ground. It was hot, scorching, like it had just fallen to Earth, and I turned it over in my hand again and again, a hypnotic motion. I glanced to my left and right. When no one was looking, I dragged the sharpest edge of the rock along a row of cars. I felt the paint give way beneath my weight. I pushed harder. Forced my hand to scrawl the letters to the worst words I could think of. Ones I would never ever say out loud.

My heart soared. Forget summer's heat, I was on fire.

"Hey!" someone called.

I dropped the rock and bolted. I ran so fast my whole chest stung. I didn't stop until I made it back to the carnival. I skirted around the Orbitron but sprinted past all the other big rides, those huge vibrating machines of flashing lights and horror. The noises they made deafened me, all that high-decibel rumbling and clattering-whooshing-grinding intermingled with a piped-in sound track of throbbing rock music. I thought I heard people yelling like they were coming after me, but when I turned to look, no one was there. I breathed a sigh of relief. Escape felt good.

Coming into a crowded food area, I eased to a walk. My fingers went to my pocket, reassuring me I hadn't lost all my money to that jerk of a carny. I found a drink stand and shoved some cash at the girl working there. I walked away with a frozen lemonade and headed toward an empty picnic table.

I sat and soaked up the night. My pulse slowed and the memory of the parking lot swirled through my mind, hazy and irretrievable like a lost balloon. Had I really done that? Written those awful things? Or had I just thought about doing it?

I didn't know. I didn't care.

A weak breeze rustled in, mussing my hair and offering a flickering moment of relief from the night's swelter. I fished a scoop of crushed ice out of my cup and rubbed it against the back of my neck. A girl's laugh floated over. I glanced up. Two tables away from me sat Keith and Charlie.

Their backs rested against the table. It looked like they were sharing fries. Charlie laughed again, turning to Keith and tucking loose hair behind her ear. My brother had a moony expression on his face, one I'd never seen before. I half stood to go over to them, but then Keith leaned in. Brushed his lips against Charlie's cheek.

I choked. Didn't move. Couldn't. Charlie pulled back and said something. She was smiling. Then she reached out and curled her fingers with his before they ran back into the crowd together.

Way later, when Phoebe found me skulking around the midway, I had murder in mind.

"What's up?" she asked.

I shrugged.

"You look upset."

"Do I?"

"Yeah, you do." She stared with those big bug eyes of hers until I relented.

"Keith and Charlie were holding hands."

She thought about this. "So?"

"They're *cousins*. They . . ." I swallowed hard. "They kissed."

Phoebe picked at a scab on her elbow. "Okay."

"It's gross."

"Really?"

"Really."

"You know," she began as a wicked smile crept across her pale lips, "your parents are cousins. How gross is that?"

A jolt went through me. "That's not true!"

"Oh, yes, it is. My dad told me." She shrugged. "I don't think it's a big deal. You shouldn't either."

This upset me terribly. And it couldn't be true. My parents had met when my mom took one of my father's courses at the university. I knew that. It explained the big age gap between them and why my dad was always right and my mom was always wrong. But I hated the fact that Phoebe would even say such a thing.

"I'll pay you twenty bucks."

I had no clue what she was talking about. "What?"

"Twenty bucks if you go on the carousel."

"Why?"

"I want to see if you'll hurl."

"No way!"

She kept at it, which irritated me. The offer eventually rose to forty bucks, but I was nothing if not stubborn. I felt a sudden slap on my back. I looked up and saw Keith grinning at me. Charlie stood right behind him. She arched an eyebrow at me in a smug way that said, *I know what you did.*

(FUCKCOCKSUCKASSHOLEBITCHCUNT)

My cheeks went hot.

Keith pointed at the spinning carousel.

"Don't do it!" he shouted.

chapter nineteen

matter

Lex sees me preparing to leave Eden. He leaps up to block my path.

"Where're you going?"

I duck around him. He hasn't earned my response.

The way he grabs for my arm feels desperate. "You can't leave, man. I mean it."

"I thought you didn't want to be anywhere near me tonight!"

His voice lowers. "Look, earlier, what I said, when you were with that girl—it came out all wrong."

"I guess it did."

"Come on. I really don't think you should be alone. Not now."

I can't help but pause. This is so unfair. Out of everyone in the entire world, how can it be that Lex Emil is the only one who knows? It's a cruel joke, and I hate irony more than anything. I really do.

Through gritted teeth, I manage, "Why do you say that?"

His eyes are so pale that as the moonlight catches them, they appear near white. Like the center of the hottest flame. "Just stay with me, Win. It's a long time until morning."

That doesn't answer my question. But in the same way I couldn't voluntarily break away from Jordan earlier, I can't walk away from Lex. Neither of us looks at the other. We're both looking at the moon. It's the celestial twin to the large stone sitting right inside my gut. Only my inner moon refuses to wax and wane. It's taken on an orbit of its own, rotating in toward my core, slowly anchoring me to the ground.

"Come on," Lex says finally. "You need a drink."

It's a command, not a request.

"You know I don't do that."

"I know you don't do a lot of things," he says. "Don't be an asshole. Tonight of all nights is when you should be letting your guard down. Releasing those inhibitions. Being *free* for once."

"I see."

"You should try hooking up, too, you know. There are some girls over there"—he jabs his thumb back toward the party—"that would love to get a shot at you. They think you're cute but aloof or some bullshit. Apparently being a douche passes for sex appeal these days. Fucking girls, how do they work, am I right?" His thundering guffaw rolls across Eden. Lex is always one to laugh at his own jokes, but this time I can tell he's forcing it.

"How about that drink?" I say.

"Oh, absolutely," he replies. "Let's do it."

"Just one."

He begins to walk back toward the music. The laughter. The voices. I'm glad we don't head for the bonfire because Jordan is still there. I'm watching her. She's gotten another beer and moved beside a group of other juniors headed up by Penn Riggsdale. Poor girl. They won't straight-up ignore her or anything, but really, she's barking up the wrong tree. Riggsdale and his crowd are Manhattan trust fund kids. The elite. The entitled. The annoying-as-hell.

I think of the way they'll laugh at Jordan when she's out of earshot. The jokes they'll make about her family. Her lack of money. Her lack of status. Her lack of beauty. She's low value to the kind of people who care about stuff like that. Good only for cracks about paper bags or affirmative action and turning dykes straight.

I'm ashamed of the way I spoke to her earlier. I should have been nicer.

"Can't you stop thinking how you're better than everyone else for like one goddamn second?" Lex asks.

I tighten my jaw. "Not likely."

"See, this is why I hate you sometimes."

Well, I thought he hated me all of the time, so I definitely take note of the qualifier. I also change the subject. I point at the bottle of liquor he's holding. Brown liquid. Economy-sized. The script on the label is supposed to be old-fashioned and classy, but how classy can a drink be when it's got a name like Early Times? I feel ill looking at it, and the stress of how it will affect my training is so not worth it, but I snatch a red plastic cup from the stack on the card table and hold it out.

Lex tips the whiskey in.

"Enough," I bark, but he keeps pouring until I yank the cup away. Early Times splashes off our shoes. Lex gives a whoop of laughter.

"Sloppy already, Winters. I'm liking your style tonight.

C'mon. Cheers." He bumps the bottle to my cup, leading to more splashing and, well, I know the drill. I tip the cup back and swallow.

Terrible. It's absolutely terrible. I hold my composure and manage not to gag or cough or curse even though I want to do all three. A lit fuse runs from my sinuses to the bottom of my stomach. I should have held out for a shot of Pucker. Or strychnine.

Lex watches me closely. "More," he says, so I drink more. But something goes wrong. It's too much or too strong or I swallow too much air. Before I know what's happening, I throw up on the ground.

People around us clap and cheer, as if my throwing up means they're having a good time. My cheeks burn, but I'm uncomfortable more than embarrassed because it still feels like there's a bubble stuck in my windpipe. I'm afraid if I try to belch it out, I'll just end up retching again.

Lex should be the one laughing the loudest and cracking jokes. That's what he's always done. That's who he's always been. But instead he's putting his hand on my back, keeping me balanced, asking, "You okay, man?"

I wave a hand. "Yeah. I'm fine."

"You really don't drink. I always forget. I'm sorry."

Those last two words stun me. I lift my head, expecting to see him smirking or holding his camera up. He looks totally serious, though. No hint of humor. Just genuine concern.

I make a fist and pound my chest to clear my throat.

"I'm fine," I repeat.

"Let's go in there." Lex points and starts walking. I follow his line of sight. He's gesturing to one of the tents. I kick dirt over the puke, then jog after him, still holding on to my empty cup.

"I'm not having sex with you," I tell him.

He shakes his head. "Dream on, Winters. Look, I'm wasted. If I don't sit and chill, I'm gonna do something stupid like tea-bag Donald Trump or hit on your girlfriend again." Donald Trump's what the whole school calls Cal Beckett, our resident young Republican and capitalist cheerleader.

"She's not my girlfriend," I say.

"Whatever. Your processing chip is shorting out again. Your capacity to detect my, admittedly lame, humor has been seriously compromised."

"Excuse me?"

"You're an idiot for how smart you are."

"I'm leaving," I say firmly, veering off-path from the tent.

"No!" barks Lex, lunging at me, tackling me around my neck so that he practically drags me to the dirt. "God, you're touchy, too. Just hang with me for a few minutes. Okay? I don't want to, you know, pass out"—he runs his hand through his hair—"or something."

This, this, what I'm feeling right now, the racing pulse, the sweating palms, the burrowing dread, *this* is anxiety. And unlike Teddy's, it's well earned. It's not a true flashback. I have plenty of those, so I know the difference. No, this is a mere memory, brief but vivid. I awake in the middle of the night. It's April of our sophomore year, just six months earlier, and a late snow falls outside, a soft dusting to cover the icy mantle beneath. The radiator blasts. The air is filled with the hiss and thump of steam rising through metal. My clothes stick to me and there's so much sweat I feel feverish. I roll over and remember what I've done and how I've betrayed Lex. Somewhere inside I ought to feel guilt or shame for my actions, but instead I'm numb.

My eyes adjust to darkness and I see the shape on the floor, near my desk. It's indistinct at first, but then I know it's him.

Lex was way drunk when I went to sleep, and now he's passed out. This is typical. There's an awful stench in the air like puke or worse, and I swear, if he's pissed his bed again, I'm moving out for good. I switch on the light and the horror of what I see strikes me all at once, but it can't truly cut through the numbness. Nothing can. I force myself to leap from bed and nudge him, but his body just flops in a weird way. His whole face is slack. His breath is shallow, almost nonexistent. And then it's happening again. It's like when they pulled my family from the water and tried to revive the dead, and now this, this part *is* a flashback. The way my teeth chatter and my eyes roll back and I can't keep the words, the horror, from slipping from my lips *ohgodohgod ohsiobhan notyou pleasepleaseplease* but I can't stop and lose my mind, not even for a second, because while they're dead and gone, Lex isn't. Not yet. Not if I can save him.

My ears roar again and now I'm a goddamn time traveler because I'm back here, on a Vermont mountaintop, with a high school party raging on around me, but I can't remember if I'm in the present or the past.

I'm split. I'm torn.

I am both ever evolving and ever decaying.

Finally, I decide I'm in the present because that's the easiest answer, but it's not like there's any real way to tell. Present me walks in the tall grass with Lex Emil, full of my usual self-assurance and swagger. I'm lean, tall, and bathed in the warm caress of moonlight, but when I look around, I can see that I'm also in the past.

Past me stands off to the side, and I am not all there. I am transparent, undefined, and charged with constant pain. I know what Lex wants to talk about. I know why he's being nice all of a sudden. It's so obvious. It's a trap. But past Win can only watch. He cannot be seen. He cannot talk to present Win

because that would disrupt things. That would have meaning-
ful consequences for the future.

Lex holds the tent flap open. He nods at present Win.

"Hurry up," he calls.

chapter
twenty

antimatter

I was already in a foul mood the morning my father showed up.
Keith and Charlie had snuck away the previous evening and
taken the train into Boston without telling me. Phoebe was the
one who let me know where they'd gone when I called over to
her house looking for him. Keith slunk back in after midnight
with his hair all rumpled and promptly kicked me out of his
bed, where I'd finally fallen asleep. I tried asking him about our
parents, about what Phoebe had said to me the night of the
carnival, but he just told me to shut it. Then he turned his back
on me.

But I knew something was up the moment I pulled on my
tennis clothes and court shoes and skipped down the back stairs

to the kitchen. Instead of encountering a quiet, darkened room, flipping on the overhead light, and scrounging for something to eat, I padded into a kitchen where two figures stood talking.

I balked. The lack of sunlight draped the room with a frigid atmosphere, and deep shadows stretched from every corner. But I knew those voices.

"Dad," I said meekly. He stood beside my grandfather. I hadn't seen him in weeks. Yet nothing had changed.

"Drew." His long fingers drummed against the bottom of his coffee mug. An ominous tattoo. A tropic storm of unease gathered inside of me. I began to sweat.

"I d-didn't know you were coming," I said.

"I wanted to surprise you."

My voice didn't sound right. My mouth felt cottony with sleep. I walked to the refrigerator to get some orange juice. My father stepped in front of me, blocking my path.

"We're going to be taking a trip in a little while."

"A trip?"

"To New Hampshire," said my grandfather, standing there in one of his ridiculous dresses. He referred to them as "sleeping gowns," but they were definitely dresses. "We've got a cabin in the White Mountains. Half mile from Crater Lake. Beautiful spot. Whole family stays up there every summer."

"New Hampshire?" I squeaked.

Two generations of restrained Winters males stared at me in silence. From the corner of my eye, I made out my Phenergan prescription sitting on the countertop, and the storm inside my head took on strength. My mind flooded with a wild blackness. I hated that they had been talking about me, planning how to get me to Crater Lake. And now no one was going to let me have breakfast. I knew it. Something snapped within me, some internal racket string that'd been wound far too tight, for far too long.

"I'm not going."

"What?"

I said it louder. "I'm *not* going!"

My grandfather gave a low laugh. A *you don't know anything* laugh.

Cheeks flushed hot, I stormed from the kitchen to the living room, where I threw myself onto an antique love seat that creaked beneath my weight. I buried my face in the musty seat cushions like an ostrich.

They followed me. Even worse, my grandmother thudded down the stairs to join them. I heard her ask my father in one of those hushed tones she usually reserved for finding out the neighbors were gay or had garden gnomes or spoke English as a second language, "Winston, what on *earth* is going on?"

When I looked up, they'd crowded around me. Waves of their displeasure and impatience washed over me. I had no room to breathe. I had no room to think. They closed in tighter, trapping me with their claustrophobic contempt. I saw my grandfather stretch out an arm to reach for me, and I knew he had the Phenergan in his other hand. In one frenzied motion I sprang from the couch, cracking the top of my head against my grandmother's chin as I did so. She reeled backward with a bleat of horror. I darted to the right, scrambling into the formal dining room and diving beneath the table onto all fours.

"Drew!" my father bellowed, his fury, humiliation, and utter confusion embedded in that one word. He thundered after me, hot on my heels, reaching under the table and grabbing for my legs. Too late. With a panicked cry, I came out the other side and launched straight for my grandmother's cherrywood hutch. My body crashed against the cabinet with a thud. The whole thing shook and rocked forward. Pieces of crystal and china rained down on top of me. I slip-crawled across piles of broken glass as wild, gasping sobs poured from deep inside my body, then I wedged myself beneath an antique secretary resting against the far wall. When I looked down, a long, crescent-shaped shard of glass was grasped between the fingers of my right hand. I brought my arm up. Pulled the shard across my own throat. Then I reached up to do it again.

"Stop!" Something grabbed hold of my arm. "Stop that!"

I shrieked and bucked backward but had nowhere to go. My left shoulder drove into the wall and I writhed like a creature in a petri dish.

"Drew, Drew," said a voice. "What are you doing?"

I blinked and looked into Keith's frightened eyes. My sides heaved. I released a strange moan of anguish, the cry of a wounded animal.

His soft words coaxed me out from under the secretary. I dropped the glass and flopped forward onto the Oriental rug like a dead fish. Keith rolled me over and pressed a napkin to my throat, which felt very warm and sticky. Then he put both arms around me and held me in his lap. I shut my eyes. His heart thumped through his T-shirt. He smelled ripe with sweat and fear, but everything, all of him, soothed me until I ached to be absorbed into his body, like one of those vanishing twins. At last, Keith said, "They're all gone, okay? I told them to leave you alone. Why don't we sit down? I'll get a bandage for the cut."

I followed him to the living room on shaky legs, surveying the mess in the dining room as I walked. What had I done? What would happen to me? This wasn't like the carnival parking lot. I had no means of escape. I moaned again. Keith settled me onto the love seat, flipped on a floor lamp, and examined my neck. His shirt was streaked with blood.

"The cuts aren't too deep. I'll be right back," he said. "Do you need anything?"

I sniffled. "Some—some orange juice."

He nodded. When he returned, he had a first aid kit and the glass of juice.

"Lean back into the light," he said, and I did. The Bactine he put on stung, but I stayed very still. A funny feeling came over me as he cleaned me and positioned the bandage and tape. The feeling started at the top of my head and worked its way down, a gauzy tingling that spread across my face and stitched up the holes in my heart, my arms, my belly. It felt good. A radiating warmth born from his touch. His concern.

At last Keith sat back. He pulled me to sitting. "They're barely more than scratches. Nothing bad. You're lucky."

I nodded. Relief flooded into his eyes, I saw it, but with the funny warm feeling gone, I felt nothing. Keith sat beside me and touched my hand and asked me what was wrong. That did it. The floodgates opened. Once I started talking, I couldn't stop. I told him everything, a great endless rush of complaints. I told him about my misery, how I was lonely, how I was jealous of Charlie, how I knew people didn't like me, how I didn't like me, no, no, not one bit. After a while, my head began to swim, a slippery sliding in and out of reality. I looked at the empty juice glass, then back at Keith. This was not a new feeling. I forced my mouth to move. "Phenergan?"

His face drooped with guilt. "Xanax, too, okay, so don't be scared. You won't remember anything."

Drugs hit me hard. Always. I started to drool and shake. Keith wrapped me in his arms again, very tight, and whispered, "I had to. I'm sorry. I told them it wouldn't be as bad if I did it. Please forgive me."

chapter
twenty-one

matter

"I know what you're waiting for." Lex lies on his left side with his elbow digging into the tent's nylon floor. His other hand plays with a pack of Marlboros, but he doesn't light up. He knows I hate cigarettes. A camping lantern hanging from a plastic hook shoots a clammy glow across his face, but above us both the tent ceiling has a cutaway that opens to the sky. I sit cross-legged and stare out at the stars. The moon hides. It's crab-crawled around the side of the mountain and I'd have to step back outside to see it.

"Yes," I say. I don't have the strength to lie or play games.

"Why tonight?" he asks.

"The moon is full."

"Yeah. I *get* that. But you—it, it hasn't happened before, has it?"

I hesitate. "N-no."

"No? Or you don't know."

"No," I say. "I haven't changed." My voice is firm and Lex nods, seeming to take my response at face value, but in truth, I'm not really all that sure. I mean, there's that guy who was killed in the woods. I still haven't heard any update on the autopsy report. If it turns out he died during the last full moon, well, maybe *I* did that instead of this unknown wild animal. Maybe I just don't remember. That's the problem with being estranged from my family, practically disowned. No one can answer my questions or tell me what to expect. I'm alone and I don't understand myself. My throat tightens. I wish I had my older brother. I wish I could talk to him, but I have to push that away. Wishes like that are selfish.

I'm selfish.

"Can I ask you something, Win?" Lex whispers.

"Sure."

"The night you told me about your family . . ."

"What about it?" I ask.

"You said it was your brother who explained it to you?"

"Yes."

"Why him?"

"He was older than me. I think it was his, you know, job to teach me."

"Why not your father?"

My back curls and the hairs on my forearms rise.

"It was my brother's job," I repeat.

"So you were close with your brother?"

"Of course."

"But he never, you know?"

"No. He never changed. He was only fourteen. He didn't get to."

"Then how do you know what he was?"

My face turns hot, my stomach, violent, but I look right at him. "You really need to back off talking about my brother, Lex. I mean it. You of all people should know better."

His eyes widen and his lips frown. The last time Lex and I talked about my brother was the night he almost died. He couldn't handle it then and he shouldn't bring it up now.

I continue to stare. I want power. I want the upper hand. I want to see the fear again on Lex's face, like I did when I was on top of him in the biology lab. But I don't. I see pity. I see sorrow.

"Win," he says quietly and with more sincerity than I would ever have believed him capable of, "what if you don't change tonight?"

There are wants and needs in this world, I think. There are hopes and guarantees. There are the things that are true and the things we need to believe in. And I've seen enough in my life to know I don't believe in much. But I do not waver in the words I say to Lex:

"I will."

chapter
twenty-two

antimatter

Mind followed body.

First my eyes opened.

Then the fear sluiced through me.

I did not know where I was.

The view from the window on the opposite wall pulled me from the unfamiliar bed where I lay. But I stood too quickly. My head became a buzzing cloud. I swayed, came close to falling, but the dizziness cleared. I walked across the room and gazed outside.

It came back to me in a tumbling rush. I was in New Hampshire, the White Mountains. That made sense. Everywhere, all I saw were trees and steep angles. A certain alpine grace. I reached out, unlatched the window, and let in the breeze. No mugginess. It felt good. I began to hum, an old jukebox song springing into my head without warning.

"Hey," a voice said. "You're up."

I turned to see Phoebe. She leaned against the doorway, one matchstick leg hooked over the other like a 4. The end of a lollipop stick jutted from her mouth, and her lips were stained red.

"Hiya," she said.

I ignored her and took my first look around the room. It had a nautical theme. There was white wicker furniture and a framed display of knots hanging on the bare wood walls. A blue rug in the shape of an anchor covered the middle of the floor. A second door stood to my right. I peeked. It was a bathroom.

"Excuse me," I said to Phoebe. My bladder hurt. I ducked in, shut the door, and stood over the toilet for a really long time. After flushing, I went to the mirror.

Ugh. I looked terrible, with drooping bags beneath my eyes and cracked lips. I ran my fingers over the neck bandages. Those, along with my matted hair, pushed me into mental patient territory. I swallowed hard. Well, considering what I'd done, I guess that wasn't so far from the truth. I'd totally lost it. The glass. The blood.

I walked out of the bathroom and crawled onto the bed. Maybe I could will my life away with sleep. Wake up a different person. This was one of my common wishes, along with discovering the power of invisibility and winning a grand slam title. Phoebe crept over to peer down at me. Her hair had been braided in a way that showed off her enormous ears.

"You okay?" she asked in a hushed voice.

"*No.* Gram is going to kill me. I broke a bunch of stuff in her house."

"I heard about that. You went seriously apeshit."

I pursed my lips. Phoebe was right, but I didn't approve of swearing.

"Yeah, well," I said. "I think I'm crazy."

"Hey," she offered. "At least you didn't get carsick on the way up."

I squeezed my knees. "That was kind of the point, wasn't it?"

"Mmm, maybe that was only part of the point."

"What do you mean?"

She didn't answer. Her face looked paler than usual. She shivered in a restless kind of way and began cruising around the room, touching things.

"Wait," I said. "What are you doing here?"

Phoebe's eyes widened. "We're all here. My family. Gram and Grandpa. Your dad."

"Oh."

"Phoebe." This came from Keith, who'd stepped in without knocking.

I tensed at the sight of him. Phoebe streaked from the room like a cat.

Keith came and sat beside me. I retreated into the corner of the bed with my back against the wall. Despite his familiar "Got Soy?" T-shirt, I hardly recognized him. He didn't look like my brother. Downy hair coated his arms and legs, and his eyes, which had always been the same dull brown as mine, had taken on the coppery tone of his hair. Fiery sparks of red floated in the irises. His strangeness felt untrustworthy. But when Keith looked right at me, I softened.

"Drew, you really scared me."

I continued to watch him.

"Why did you cut yourself like that?" he asked.

I wanted to die.

"I don't know," I said.

I didn't react when I saw his tears well up like a summer

storm. Not until they spilled over, ran down his cheeks, and mixed with his snot. Then I got scared and felt a desperate lump build in my own throat. I didn't want to have to comfort him. I didn't know *how*.

"God, Drew, just—just don't do anything like that again. Come to me if you're sad, all right? Or angry. I love you, I can't watch you hurt yourself."

I crept forward and laid my head on his shoulder. I felt horrible. Black guilt pinched my flesh. Everywhere. Hard.

Keith said, "I'm sorry."

I didn't know how to respond. *I* was the one who felt sorry. Not in the apology kind of way. In the I-hate-myself-and-deserve-to-suffer kind of way.

"Come on," he directed. "Let's go for a walk."

The muscles in my gut tightened as Keith and I left the bedroom and walked down the hall. I half expected my grandmother to jump out and hit me again. But she didn't. We stepped outside without incident.

The sky was brilliantly clear, a turquoise template of summer. The surface of a nearby lake sparkled at us through the trees.

I breathed deeply, inhaling mountain air and sweet, sweet relief. I'd escaped punishment. For now.

Keith read my mind. "Everyone's down at the water. Grandpa got a new boat or something, and I said I'd stay with you. I don't get why Phoebe decided to stick around."

She wants to spy on us, I thought, but said nothing. I looked back and gaped at the cabin. Actually, cabin wasn't a big enough word. The place loomed like a castle, all stone and glass, reminding me of the photographs my mom had shown me of Ireland, the lush mountains where she'd grown up, ones that looked like a different world. I turned and followed my brother. He led us into the woods, away from the water.

"You know," Keith said as we walked, "I haven't done right by you, Drew. I'm sorry for that."

I thought of him and Charlie, all their sneaking around. I nodded. Around us, trees closed in. Everything grew darker. Colder.

"A long time ago, when you were just a little kid, I promised myself I would always take care of you. Siobhan, too. It's like, I was put here to protect you two, because Mom won't. Or can't. Or isn't strong enough or whatever."

I nodded again, not wanting to think about our mom, who could be cold and distant in ways that made me feel empty. Instead I pictured Siobhan, with her pigtails and her laughter and her eternal smile. But even that image stung, burning some tender part of me. I remembered how I liked my sister so much more than Phoebe, because Phoebe was rude and never listened to anything I said.

I glanced up. Keith was staring right at me.

"I'm hungry," I said. The words came out whinier than I intended.

He reached into the pocket of his nylon shorts and handed me a package of orange crackers and orange cheese. I tore the plastic too hard and the flat red spoon went flying. I didn't see where it landed, so I used my finger to get at the cheese.

"Don't you worry about her?" Keith asked softly.

"Yes," I said, although I wasn't sure who he was talking about anymore. Siobhan? Phoebe? The only girl who *worried* me was Charlie. She'd single-handedly ruined my brother. Ruined this entire crummy summer. But I couldn't say that. I needed Keith back on my side, and to get him, I had to agree with him. I had to show him I could be cooler than some long-legged girl whose butt wiggled when she walked.

We pressed through an alder thicket. And beyond. More dark. More cold. Above and on every side. Vines and branches grabbed at my shirt and bare legs. The eggy stink of a peat bog hit me. I pinched my nose tight.

"I should have told you he was coming. I know that. Seeing him like that wasn't fair to you. But I've been . . . preoccupied. So I'm sorry. Really sorry. This morning, I guess I didn't think about how upset you'd be to see him."

Why did Keith sound so shrill? I put all my attention into watching the way his mouth moved as he spoke. His thin lips. That mole between his nose and cheek. The sun backlit him in such a way that if I blurred my focus, he reminded me of a talking moose.

Keith swallowed hard. Gasped for air. "I've wanted to talk to you about it for so long. It's the reason I arranged for you to come away with me this summer. But it's not easy. It's not. It's the kind of thing that eats away at you. Secrets are toxic, you know? But it's not you, Drew. I need you to know that. It's not your fault. I tried so hard to protect you. But I couldn't. And last summer when—"

The grunting of the bullfrogs drowned out the rest of his words. That was unfortunate. Keith had asked a question or said something important. I was sure of it.

"Did you even hear what I said?" Keith hissed.

I sidestepped through mud. My feet stuck to the ground and made sucking noises as I forced them free. "Uh, yeah, I heard you."

"Did you ever talk about it with your counselor?"

"My counselor?"

"The one you got sent to last year."

"Did we talk about Soren?"

Keith stared at me. "Not *Soren*. What happened before. With *Dad*."

Before.

Ssssnap!
nevertelldrew
promiseme
"Oh," I said.

"So you didn't talk about it?"

"I—I don't remember."

"You don't remember what happened or you don't remember if you talked about it?"

"I don't know!" I stuffed the rest of the crackers into my mouth. Why didn't he just tell me what he wanted me to say? Speculation was not in my nature. Reaction was. I peeked over. Keith was crying again, like full-out sobs that made his whole body shake.

The high-pitched trill of a tree frog drew me in. I inched to the very edge of the swamp before I saw it, a summer peeper, bright green with brown spots. It sat on a moss-draped trunk and sang to me.

I tried singing back.

Tiny bubbles . . .

Keith yanked me around by the sleeve, a violent motion, until I faced him again. "Damn it! You can't do this. It's what you always do."

What was?

"You have to have some sort of reaction, Drew. This shutting-down thing of yours, the spacing out, it's bullshit!"

"Bullshit," I echoed. I leaned around him to see the frog again, but it had hopped away.

"We can't change what happened, but we can change ourselves if we talk about it. Look how messed up we are already! Half the time I feel like I can't breathe, you know? Like someone's stomping around on top of my chest. It *hurts.* And you, you're always so angry. The way you're always fighting. How you don't have any friends. You're like a bomb waiting to go off, I know you are!" He ran his hand through his thick hair. More sobs escaped him.

An alarm bell went off in my head. Uh-oh. Did he know about those cars I'd scratched up? The bad words I'd written? Would I go to jail?

Keith's nostrils flared. A sick fervor gleamed in his eyes. "Remember those wolves we saw last year, Drew? Their pack mentality? That guy, he said the lone wolves usually die, so you can't be a lone wolf, all right? We're like that pack. We have to stick together, no matter what. Promise me that."

"I promise," I said quickly, although I didn't understand what he was talking about. Wolves and bombs? I felt jumpy and uncomfortable, as if I'd begun to leave my own body, as if I had a leaky soul. The words I'd said to Phoebe ran through my head: *I think I'm crazy*. But new words came to me, like a second language. *I think Keith is crazy, too.*

"You know what scares me the most?" His voice dropped, morphing into a low whine that joined with the drone of the dragonflies hovering above the bog. "That we might become the same way. That *we'll* hurt people, too. I learned about it in school and I read about it online. This kind of thing, this *sickness*, it probably happened to him when he was a kid. Maybe Grandpa did it . . . and now it's—it's like a cycle that gets passed down from one generation to the next. Unless we stop it."

He was starting to sound weird, like creepy weird. I had to do something. I had to change the subject.

"Hey, Keith, are Mom and Dad related? Like cousins or something?"

Keith took a deep breath and shook his head. "No. What're you talking about? Where'd you hear that?"

"I dunno. Someone said something to me."

"Well, forget about that. It's stupid. I'm trying to talk to you—"

"What about you and Charlie? You're cousins. Is that stupid, too?"

His face went bright red. "Jeez, just shut up already, Drew."

"Don't tell me to shut up! I've seen you two. Like at the fair, you *kissed* her!"

Keith's mouth opened. Then closed. "You don't know what you're talking about. At all."

"Well, I don't like her. I think she's bad for you to be around."

He snorted. "No, she's not."

"She's mean," I said. "She's mean to me."

"You know, your precious Anna is the one to watch out for. She's the bad one."

"No, she isn't!" My voice rose. It startled me.

"Yeah, right," said Keith.

"What about you?" I snapped back.

"What about me?"

"You're the meanest of all! You're the one who drugged me!"

Keith's jaw dropped. A great cloud of hurt and shock blew across his face.

"*Drew,*" he said, reaching for me.

Then it was the hunger, the thirst, the medication, the stress, I don't know, but I didn't feel well. My legs buckled right there in the cool shade of the mossy forest. Keith must have seen something, the sickly gray of my cheeks, the vacant glaze of my eyes, because he grabbed me around the chest before I pitched over.

"I have to lie down," I managed.

"We'll head back." He leaned down. "Get on."

I rode on his back the rest of the way. I wrapped my arms around his shoulders and turned my head to watch the forest go by above me. A surreal effect, it felt like the world had been flipped. I floated, weightless, nothing more than ether pulled into a formless journey. The dark branches of the trees swept us along, long, shadowy arms raking against our bodies, propelling us forward. That flutter of fear riffled through me again. I squeezed my eyes shut.

I focused on the rhythmic sway of my brother's body as he carried me.

I focused on the whispering of the trees.

Wolves and bombs, the trees said, and my stomach turned over.

I felt unbalanced.

Where, wolf? I thought madly.

Whither wolf, Keith?

chapter
twenty-three

matter

I decide the best defense is a good offense. It's a common strategy of mine.

"Teddy's worried about you," I tell Lex.

He lets his head fall back with a loud sigh. "So what else is new? Teddy's worried about *everything*."

"Yeah. But the day after that guy was found in the woods, he told me you knew him."

Lex snorts. "Teddy really told you that?"

"Yes."

"Whatever."

"He also says you've been drinking too much," I add.

"Whoa, wait. *Why* did Teddy tell you all of this?"

"Because he couldn't find you. He thought I might know where you were."

"Oh, right. See, now I know you're lying, Win. Why on earth would Teddy ever think that?"

Lex is good. Really good. Clearly, I need to offer up something first if I expect to get anything in return. "Because he saw me eavesdropping on the cops. The morning they found that guy's body."

"Well, now we're getting somewhere. Why were you eavesdropping?"

I feel flustered. "I was just curious."

"Awesome. So Teddy's worried. And you're curious. Am I getting this right?"

"I guess," I say.

"What does any of this have to do with me? Because, you know, I'm not either."

"Either what?"

Lex smirks. "Worried or curious."

"Tell me how you know the dead guy."

"Tell me why you care."

I'm playing with fire here, but I push forward. "I care because Teddy said you talked to him last April. At a party out here. The Rite of Spring. That's the same night you came back to our room and almost died."

The squeak of Lex's leather jacket as he runs his hand across his own face is the only sound inside the tent. I can't even hear him breathing. Outside there's lots of noise. Laughter. Shouting. The thudding bass and low, lazy vocals of what I think might be the Wu-Tang Clan.

I'm not breathing either. The space between us is inconsequential. It's inches, maybe. Or feet. Nothing hangs between us. Just air molecules. Oxygen. Nitrogen.

In other ways, the space between us is immeasurable.

"Almost died," Lex repeats softly.

"That's what the ER doc said. That your central nervous system was shutting down when you came in."

"Okay."

"He thought you did it on purpose, you know. Mixed stuff. Alcohol. Vicodin."

"Is that what you think?"

"I don't know. It was, you know, after we talked," I say.

Lex narrows his eyes. "Why would what we talked about make me want to kill myself?"

"You were upset."

"Oh fuck, Win. Fuck. I can't believe you're bringing this up like this. I can't believe it."

"What?"

"You're acting like your *talking* is what upset me. Did you somehow manage to forget the part of that night where you *totally screwed me over*?"

I swallow. "No."

He points a finger at me. "Because if I wanted to *die*, there's no way in hell I would do it with something lame like sleeping pills. Man, I'd do it right. I'd use a gun or jump off a—" He stops.

I continue to hold my breath. My lungs ache-burn, but I don't give in. I need the hurt. I do. I need some kind of present-day suffering in order to hold the past pain at bay. The memory of Siobhan's honey hair fluttering as if waving good-bye. The urgent howl of the train whistle.

"Oh, shit," Lex says. "I'm sorry. I'm so sorry. I am such an idiot sometimes."

I say nothing.

He keeps talking. "This is . . . you're right. I *don't* know if I can deal with this. I really don't. I thought I could, and I'm the one who wanted to talk to you tonight. I mean, I'm over what happened with Kelsey, I really am. And the way I've acted these last few months, it's never been about that. It's more that . . . look, I know I've been a real dick. I can't even, you know, apologize for that. I just *am* a dick sometimes. It's who I am. I don't know why. I don't have a good reason. I guess I tried to convince myself that it was funny to screw around with you. Because I was mad and, well, because you have such a stick up your ass sometimes, Win, you really do."

I exhale. "Thanks."

"But after the other day, in the biology lab, it struck me how serious you are with all this. So none of it's funny anymore. It's fucking sad. And I'm sorry that I handled things like I did back then. I mean, yeah, I was pissed you screwed around with the girl I liked, but after you told me, after you explained, well, I should have—" His voice cracks. He shakes his head more. Stuffs his fist into his mouth to keep the words from coming out.

I am confused. His show of emotion repulses me. Is he apologizing for being weak? Maybe he remembers that night differently from the way I do. In fact, I'm sure he does. He was drunk and angry, and after I went to sleep, he took a bunch of Vicodin. And he did it on purpose. I know that, even if he doesn't. I was the clearheaded one that night, but we've never talked about it since. So it stands to reason he might not remember things accurately.

"You need help, Win," he says.

I smile. "Tell me how you knew the dead guy."

Lex's mouth gapes. "Are you listening to me?"

"I'm listening to you avoid my questions."

"Oh, wow. I'm not avoiding *anything*. Okay, I knew him because I bought drugs off him. Stupid, yeah, but that's it. He was a dealer, my hookup, small-time stuff. I invited him. He bought the booze for us. That's why he was at that party. Now the dumb-ass went and got himself mauled by a bear or a moose or a rabid badger, go figure. This is Vermont. It happens all the time. Who the fuck cares?"

"The drugs you took that night?"

Lex throws his hands in the air, exasperated. "Yes. Happy? It's all totally irrelevant. Why are we talking about me? This is about you. You should, you know, talk to somebody. I'm serious. And it takes a hell of a lot for me to say that. I don't believe in crap like that. Talking about emotions or taking meds when life gets hard, you know?"

"That's ironic."

"Fuck if I care," he snaps bitterly. "What I mean is that I lived with you for two years. I didn't say anything when you had those nightmares. All those times you woke up screaming. I didn't care that you used to do that shit like hit yourself or stick your finger down your throat or whatever. I *protected* you."

"Teddy says you've been drinking too much."

He holds his hand up. "Just stop."

"What?"

"Stop making this about *me*! Look, when I needed help, you helped me. And when you needed it, I bailed. I did worse than that. I treated you like shit. So just let me help you, okay?"

"What do I need help with?"

"You told me there's a wolf inside of you."

"Yes," I breathe.

"That's crazy, Win."

"No, no, it isn't," I say.

"How can that be?"

How can it not?

"It just is. I know. I *feel* it."

"Then why haven't you changed?"

"I'm going to. It's just, I've been . . ." I choose my words carefully. "Stressed."

Lex sighs. "Well, explain it to me, then. Why you? I mean, I'm not a wolf."

"Genetics. I don't understand it all, but it must be some kind of mutation or a recessive thing. I'm pretty sure it's linked to hormones and physical development, like puberty, you know? But maybe the stress hormones are holding me back. Cortisol can do that. Alter metabolism. Delay maturity."

"You have an answer for everything."

"I've done a lot of reading on the topic."

Lex pauses. "You know, you also told me what happened with your brother and your sister. How they died. Why you changed your name."

Even though Lex didn't ask a direct question, I also have an answer for that. I really do. I have all the right words. But when my mouth opens, my vocal cords freeze. Nothing comes out.

Nothing.

chapter
twenty-four

antimatter

"Drink this." Keith set a glass on the counter in front of me. We'd just returned from our hike.

I shot him a tentative glance.

"It's water," he said. The guilt in his voice was palpable. "Nothing else. I promise."

I nodded and drank it. I still felt weak. The clock on the wall said it was after four in the afternoon. An entire day had vanished.

"You hungry?" Keith asked me.

I shook my head.

"Go lie down, then, or something. Rest. You look peaky."

"What's peaky?"

"Sick."

"When will they be back?"

He shrugged. "Don't know. Why?"

"I need to tell Gram I'm s-sorry. For hitting her."

Keith rolled his eyes. "Oh, please. You don't need to tell her anything."

I felt like crying, just all of a sudden. "Is everyone mad at me?"

"No. Well, Gram started in a bit with how out of control you can be, but Dad told her to knock it off. Said you hadn't meant to break anything, that traveling was hard on you."

"He did? He said that?"

"Yup."

"What about this?" I touched my bandages.

Keith looked right at me. "I told them the cuts were an accident, okay? That's just between us. Got it?"

I nodded, slid off the bar stool, and switched on the television in the living room. *Pokémon* was on, which I liked, but when Keith came in and sat next to me with a bowl of popcorn, I changed over to a baseball game. Only the Braves weren't playing. It was the Red Sox, whom we both hated.

As the day faded, the front door opened and the rest of our family streamed in, loud, exhausted, and sunburned from hours at the lake. My grandfather and uncle both grabbed beers from the refrigerator and joined us. They were Boston fans, naturally. Charlie and Anna bounced around and talked about driving into town to see a movie because Anna had just gotten her license. My dad marched upstairs without a word or glance in my direction. My stomach started to hurt. I looked at Keith.

"It's not you," he whispered. "I think something happened while he was in New York. He got asked to leave that fellowship. That's why he's here. The only reason. So you just stay out of his way. You hear me?"

I nodded, but my body felt overinflated, like I'd been filled up from the inside. I clawed self-consciously at my chest, my neck. My skin flaked at the touch, a sloughing of dried blood and dust.

I felt filthy.

"I need to take a bath," I said, and Keith nodded, only half listening. He was trying to get Charlie's attention.

I headed back to the nautical room and entered the bathroom. I switched on the light, took my clothes off, and waited for the water to fill. The room swirled with steam. Moisture collected around my hairline.

I grimaced at my blurry reflection in the full-length mirror on the back of the door. I hated what my body looked like. I always had. Part of the problem was an umbilical hernia that my parents declined to have surgically fixed. It stuck out like a button. I poked at it and pictured a piece of my innards pushing back out, trying to escape containment.

The tub was full. I turned the tap off and stepped in. The heat felt good on my grimy skin and I sank against the tiled wall, careful not to get my bandages wet.

I closed my eyes and promptly fell asleep.

We were in agreement for once.

My dreams wanted to trick me.

I wanted to let them.

My eyes opened hours later. Day had turned night and the bathwater cold. That made me angry. Why had nobody come to check on me? I could have drowned. I'd heard of people not waking up until after they'd already slipped beneath the water. Some even died. Our neighbor Lee tried to tell me that drowning in the bathtub was just a myth, that all those people had actually been murdered by some undetectable poison; but considering the source, I had serious doubts.

Goose bumps rose across my skin as I stepped out. Wet feet on cold floor. My teeth chattered. I grabbed a towel and hustled back into the bedroom. The window remained wide open from earlier, pale curtains fluttering. I went to close it. I didn't want anyone to see in. I didn't want anyone to see me.

As I leaned forward, my gaze lit on the sight of the full moon. It hung deep in the summer sky, more amber than white.

My pulse picked up.

I heard something.

I leaned closer.

The sky was very blue and very dark, like the paint on my father's luxury sedan. I'd never seen a night like it. I kept staring. The stars twinkled back in a way that let me know they saw me, too.

I held my breath. So I *had* heard something—the language of the stars.

Listen to the moon, they said. *Listen.*

Yes.

I did not hesitate. I slid belly first out the window and into the night. I ran toward the New Hampshire forest with my bare feet slapping along the dirt trail, getting all sticky with sap and all stuck with pine needles. The towel slipped from my waist as I reached the tree line, but I didn't care. I kept going. My strange body, with its jutting bones and too-long limbs and way more height than it knew what to do with, had a mind of its own.

I set my gaze on the stars again.

The moon, they told me. *Keep going. Keep listening.*

Fear snapped at my ankles because I couldn't see the moon anymore. It sat too low, hidden by the trees. But I kept running. The stars said I had to.

I traveled deeper.

Farther.

Darker.

The trail before me rose suddenly, a steep pitch. I fell forward onto all fours and scrabbled my way up, using hands and feet like I was climbing the rock wall in the school gym. I grasped at roots and stones, and my legs struggled, working hard.

At last, I ascended.

I looked up.

A small clearing sat before me, full of swirling mist and bathed in a silver glow. I crept forward into the light and sighed, relieved.

I'd found the moon.

I sat back on my haunches. I strained to hear something, someone, anything, anyone, but my ears rang with the barren song of absolute silence.

I lifted my head, opened my throat, and howled.

And the wolves appeared.

Their eyes came first, many of them, shining in the darkness. My body thrummed with anticipation as a black wolf strode straight out of the night and came toward me. Its sable coat glimmered, warmed by the moonlight, but as the creature neared, I shrank back, seized abruptly by a choking terror. My heart pounded. This wasn't what I expected. This wasn't the type of creature I remembered from the animal preserve back in West Virginia. This was not an exotic dog or a ratty thing to be pitied.

This was a beast.

The black wolf kept coming. The oxlike power of its muscles was evident, a fine show of strength that rippled with each step. I struggled to get back onto my feet, to run, but my limbs refused to work. I knelt before it on the ground. I was naked. Exposed.

"Help me," I whispered. "Please. Oh, God!"

It reached me with its frayed, batlike ears blown back tight against its head. The animal placed one giant forepaw on either side of my body and stood above me. Its draping tail whipped back and forth. I gagged at the ripe, rotting odor coming off its fur. I bit back the scream I knew would be torn from my throat as the beast reached down with its dripping snout. But the animal merely pressed its cold nose against my cheek, an almost gentle touch, like a sickening caress. I shuddered.

More wolves came forward. They streamed from every direction. All colors. All sizes. All somehow familiar. Brown, gray, tan, white. Even a reddish beast sprang from the shadows with a snap and a snarl to strut before me, its body lithe, its movements light with grace and swagger.

I reached out with both hands and the beasts crowded in, licking-nuzzling-keening, long ears cocked low, tails held down in deference. I touched and scratched them all, not caring about the smell or the threat.

The wolves closed even tighter, tight, so tight, until I could no longer see the sky.

chapter
twenty-five

matter

I unzip the opening to the tent and stick my head out. The party looks the same, but the atmosphere in Eden is calmer. Drunker. Sleepier. But something is wrong. Upon further assessment, I realize what it is.

Jordan is missing.

My gaze darts around the campfire, always returning to the rock where we sat. She's not there. She just isn't. I pull my phone out. It's two thirty in the morning. I squint and try to make out the crowd that's playing cards near the back of the hollow, up against the cliff wall. I told her to ask Teddy to walk her back if she wanted to leave. I definitely told her that. I know I did. But Teddy's still there, slumped in his camping chair, staring at his cards with a deadly serious expression. He's not drinking. He's not high. He's no longer playing poker. He's playing Shanghai rummy. I know this because Teddy always wants to play Shanghai. It's his thing. He calls it "the mother of all card games," which I guess is pretty accurate since the game takes like five hours to finish. It's kind of fun due to all the strategy required, and I enjoy most anything where I have a fair shot at winning, but at the end of the day, it's still a card game. Nothing to lose money over. Nothing to get worked up about.

I am, however, worked up over the fact that Jordan either (a) did not listen to me and is walking through the woods alone; or (b) is in the woods, not walking and not alone. I cannot reconcile my distress with the fact that if she is alone, then she can't be in danger from *me* because, well, I'm *here*, and if she's with someone else, then that should be a good thing. Right? That's what I wanted, for her to be safe. It's what I *thought* I wanted.

Then why am I distressed?

It's confusing.

I am confused.

Lex comes up from behind. He does it slowly. He knows better than to startle me.

I'm still struggling to breathe. To speak.

"It must fucking suck," he says.

I have no clue what he's talking about. I know he's continuing our conversation, but I've lost his line of thinking. I peer around some more. The roaring in my ears is back. Jordan would remember the way down the mountain, wouldn't she? The cross-country team runs through these woods almost every day, or at least we did until this past week when the headmaster said we couldn't. No, Jordan doesn't have a flashlight, but it's not like the trails are all that complicated.

"What changed your mind?" Lex asks.

I shrink away. I still don't understand what he wants to know, but I don't think I want to tell him, either. I can't. My voice won't come to me, and that can mean only one thing: I'm scared.

"You saw them, didn't you? The bodies? I don't understand. Why didn't your parents get—"

"Is that Penn Riggsdale?" I force the words. They're explosive and my voice comes out scratchy and high-pitched in a way I don't recognize.

Lex crawls closer. He sticks his head out, too, and right, I forgot, he actually has a flashlight, a red Maglite. He pulls it from his jacket and switches it on. The beam cuts across the meadow. We both see the back of a guy walking away from us. We make out Vans. A suede jacket. Skinny jeans. A head full of dark curls. The guy isn't walking toward the trail that leads back to campus. He's heading in the opposite direction. Out of Eden and past the caves. Toward the trail that leads to the summit.

"That's him," Lex confirms.

Penn doesn't notice the flashlight. It's not strong enough. Or he's not sober enough. He turns and calls out something to his group of pretentious friends. There's a row of laughter. The sound is jarring and cruel. Penn jogs a few steps, like he's eager, too eager, and ducks out of the hollow. Out of my sight.

My body tenses like a hunting dog on point.

"Jordan," I say.

Lex looks at me. "Who?"

I repeat her name. Same tone. Same urgency. Like a chant. Or a prayer.

"That's the girl you came up with? The new one?"

I snap, "Where is she?"

"I don't know. She was over by the fire—"

"No, where is she *now*?"

His eyes widen. "What? You think Riggsdale's going to do something to her?"

I bolt.

Lex calls after me, but his efforts are a lost cause. My legs pump hard. My feet are sure-footed. I am damn fast.

Jordan.

chapter
twenty-six

antimatter

Outside, night happened. Black sky and white stars and a giant
moon.

Inside, chaos happened. The wolves were gone.

I roamed through the cabin, up and down hallways, wrapped
in towels and crying. I didn't know where I'd been or how I'd
gotten here, but I was looking for someone, anyone. I craved
closeness. I padded from room to room, calling out for Keith.
Nobody answered. Nobody stirred. A ribbon of fear stitched
through my sternum. Was anyone actually here? Had I been
abandoned?

I snuck upstairs, still crying. I longed for my dog with an
ache that almost broke me.

I knocked on the first door I found. No answer. I turned the knob and stepped in.

This room had shades, not curtains, and they were drawn. Fingers of weak moonlight squeezed through to touch the hardwood floor, but I couldn't make out anything other than a figure sleeping beneath the sheets on a pullout bed. I tiptoed as close as I could. I listened to the soft, rhythmic breathing. It did not sound familiar.

I crept closer and the sleeping figure rolled over, lifting its head. My eyes adjusted to the darkness. It was Anna. She said nothing. She didn't ask why I was there. She didn't ask why I was crying. She pulled the sheet back and beckoned me to her. I crawled into her bed and she wrapped a blanket around me. I shivered, trying to get warm. She closed her eyes, rolled away from me, and went back to sleep. My bare feet were clean, I realized, which meant everything about the wolves had been a dream, but Anna's hair was matted with sticks and dirt, which meant maybe it hadn't.

I shifted and whimpered, so confused. I tried remembering everything I could about the wolves, to hold on to them. The image of the beasts and the memory of their touch, with all their power and brute strength, flooded over me. I still felt it. That power. Inside of me. Like a great wolfish flame that sparked and burned, molten hot, at the very core of my being. It's who I was. My nature. I knew it to be true.

I remembered their roughness, too, the nipping and the fear, but Anna's words about my grandmother came back to me.

Love doesn't always look nice.

So I sighed deeply.

And suddenly, I understood everything. *Everything.*

I knew what the moon had tried to tell me in the woods.

I was not broken.

I was savage.

———

The girls took me to Crater Lake the following afternoon. Keith wouldn't talk to anyone when he woke up that morning, so he didn't come with us.

I felt bold and lay on my back in our grandfather's sailboat while it remained tied to the dock. The sun beat down crisp, bare, and the blue sky stretched forever, perfectly clear. My ears filled with the jackhammer beat of a woodpecker and the urgent buzz of racing Jet Skis.

A smattering of campsites ringed the lake, and the area swarmed with summer crowds, the inescapable scent of lighter fluid and bug spray. Beside the marina sat a public beach. It's where Phoebe walked along the rocky shore, swinging a green plastic bucket in one hand and an ancient fishing net in the other, searching for crawdads.

A blustering wind drove tiny whitecaps into the shore with a slap. The sandwich and milk I'd eaten flipped around inside me, at odds with the motion of the boat. I'd have to get out in a few minutes, but for now I liked the wildness of the feeling. The danger.

Charlie and Anna lay sunbathing side by side near the bow. The boat's mast towered over them. An American flag at the very top snapped and whipped in the breeze. Each girl wore dark sunglasses, and they passed a tiny cigarette back and forth between them. The smoke smelled weird, like the seasonings in my grandmother's lentil soup.

Charlie rolled onto her stomach, kicked her heels into the air. She pulled a small camera from her purse, gestured for me to sit up, and snapped a picture. "Come on, Drew. Tell us again about your dream."

I smiled. I crawled close to where she lay. She was being kinder toward me than she'd been all summer. Ever since I'd told her and Anna about my dream with the wolves, the two of them had fawned over me. I liked that. Keith didn't want me to go to the lake with them, but the girls insisted. They laughed and made me lunch and put sunscreen on my back.

"I think you were there, Charlie," I said, remembering the red wolf with the fearsome attitude. It felt like that wolf was the one staring at me right now.

The girls both giggled.

I thought of the other wolves. All of them. All those colors.

"Anna, you might have been there, too."

"Tell me what I looked like," Charlie said. Smoke came out of her mouth with the words.

"Very strong and fast." I squinted up at her. "It felt so real. You know, for a dream."

"Maybe it was real, little Drew," she said easily.

The hairs on my neck rose. That's exactly what I'd been thinking, that it was all real, every second. "So do you remember? Do you remember what it feels like to change? Or, you know, do you forget that?"

Charlie pressed up onto her elbows. Her sky-blue bikini looked too small for her. The soft parts of her top threatened to pop out. "Oh, I remember. It's like, totally liberating to have your body become . . . what's the word?"

Anna lay on her back. A group of young men on a passing boat whistled at her. I glared. Anna ignored them. She just put the funny cigarette up to her lips, inhaled deeply, and tossed her hair.

"Dangerous," she said.

Charlie twisted around to look at the guys. She waved wildly. "Hey, Ricky!"

A blond one leaned out over the water. "Hey, babe. When's your sister gonna let me hit it?"

She laughed. "What about me?"

"You? You're still a kid, babe."

She got to her feet. Shimmied her hips. "Do I look like a kid to you?"

He roared. "Hell, no."

The guy next to him called out, "If there's grass on the field, play ball."

Charlie lifted her middle finger.

The first guy returned the favor. They'd almost drifted past our slip. "I'm serious. You tell her I'm only up here for two more days."

Charlie sat back down and looked at Anna. "Ricky's only in town for two more days."

Anna kept her eyes pointed heavenward. "I know."

"He's cute."

"He's only after one thing."

"What's he after?" I asked.

Both girls giggled again.

"Come on," I whined.

"Ask your brother," Charlie told me.

"Ask him what?"

She pushed her glasses back. "Hasn't anyone explained sex to you?"

I swallowed hard. "Yes," I said, although this was only partially true. Sure, I knew *some* stuff, but no one had really explained anything. Not even after that embarrassing debacle in first grade when I got caught telling Siobhan she'd grown inside Mommy's tummy because Mommy ate her. Everyone laughed and no one told me the truth. But I'd seen things on the computer that had to do with sex. Things that left me feeling weak and queasy despite the fact I'd gone looking for them in the first place. Even now, as I thought about it all, my stomach hitched. I put a hand over my mouth.

"You okay?" Anna asked.

I nodded. Put my hand down.

"If you feel sick, you should try this." Charlie waved the cigarette beneath my nose. "It's medicinal, you know."

Anna kicked her in the shin. "*Don't* be stupid."

"Tell me how you knew," I said.

Charlie wriggled onto her side. "Knew what?"

Anna crawled from the boat onto the dock. Then she adjusted her suit. "I'll be right back."

Charlie didn't watch her go. She didn't take her eyes off me. Her cool gaze took in my every movement. Her wolf floated very close to the surface. I could feel it.

Nothing felt cool or composed about me. I wanted what Charlie had. I wanted her power. "You knew you were going to change, right?"

A sly smile crossed her lips. "Yes," she said.

"How?"

"It just made sense."

"So will I change?"

"Of course."

"But how will I know when it's time?"

"When you're ready, you'll know," she told me. "You really will. Your mind, your body, will tell you."

"It'll be obvious?"

"Oh, sure."

"But what does it feel like exactly? Tell me."

Charlie giggled again in her throaty way, then broke into a coughing fit. The boat bounced in the wind. I felt sickened and thrilled. I thought of the whispering trees in the forest as I rode on Keith's back. The talking stars. The moon. Could everything speak to me? Did I just need to listen?

"Drew!"

My head whipped up. Keith marched down the dock in green swim trunks and no shirt. His voice held a tone of warning.

"Drew!" he snapped again. "Get out of the damn boat."

A flush of anger washed through me. I didn't answer.

Charlie gave a languid stretch. She turned toward Keith as he approached.

"He's fine," she said, although she hastily dropped the little cigarette into the lake.

Keith saw her do it. He frowned. "He doesn't look fine. And he knows better."

I shot him a look of pure hatred.

"Don't take your anger at me out on him," Charlie called.

Keith blushed and ignored her. He jumped onto the cabin floor, causing the boat to sway wildly. He knelt on the wooden bench and reached across the bow for my arm. Just before he touched me, I leaned over and vomited up everything inside my stomach. It went all over my lap and part of Charlie's towel.

Keith waved his hands helplessly. Charlie muttered, "Nasty," and bolted from the boat, quick as lightning.

chapter
twenty-seven

matter

A little part of me hears the familiar whisper of the trees as I thunder down the hillside, across the meadow, and it's so hard to tell: Am I on two legs or four? The capacity of my heart to pump blood to every part of my body is unparalleled thanks to years of tennis, years of running, years of striving for excellence. More than one person calls my name as I streak past the bonfire, but I don't stop. I don't slow down. I round the sharp turn past the cliff wall and really put on speed as I pass the caves. It's like I've entered the bell lap of a race that really matters. A race with the highest stakes. A race in which I have everything to lose. I run faster. My lungs contract and expand.

There's no light, but I don't need it. The moon is more than enough.

If Penn hears me bearing down on him, his reflexes are too slow. He's drunk. He's high. He's horny. A strangled cry escapes me. I launch myself into the air, picturing talons and teeth, and slam against his back. Our bodies collide with a thud. We fall to the ground. I am skinny but tall. He's strong but slow. We grapple. Limbs twine. I writhe and throw punches and kick and grab and scratch. I'm yelling, but I don't know that until I realize I can't hear what Penn's yelling back. Then I wrap both hands around his throat to shut him up.

I squeeze.

Harder.

White pain explodes on the side of my face. I crumple like a felled stag and Penn wriggles away from me. He mutters, "Goddamn . . . goddamn," over and over. I lie on my side, feeling nauseated. I hear the thunder of approaching footsteps.

"What happened?"

"It's goddamn Win! He jumped Penn."

"Jesus."

"The guy's nuts. Total fucking psycho."

"Remember that stunt he pulled on the tennis court last year?"

"You good, Riggsdale? You knocked him the fuck out, didn't you?"

"Hell, yeah, I did."

I lift my head. I pant. Penn's lying, but I don't care about that. He's not the one who knocked me out. My good eye, the one that's not bleeding and impossible to open, flickers to the person standing back from the crowd. To her steel-tipped motorcycle boots with the silver buckles that flash and gleam in the night's lunar glow.

Jordan.

Her hands are on her hips. Her nostrils are flared. She's glaring right at me.

Penn's friends drag him off, back toward Eden, all while blabbing about how fucked up they are and whether or not they should just crash up here or risk sneaking back into the dorms during the night. Both plans have their pros and cons, and I can't help hoping they get busted. I have no problem saying it: I'm pissed.

As they walk away, I hear a voice say, "Dude, why do you even talk to that guy? He sucks."

"Fuck off," snaps another voice. It's Lex. He kneels beside me. "You were too fast for me, Win. Seriously. I had to miss watching you get your ass beat by Penn Riggsdale, of all people. You should've been able to take him, you know. I mean it. I hate that asshole."

I curl into a ball. The flashlight shines right in my eyes. Lex's face is like two inches from mine. His breath is awful. Cigarettes and Early Times make for an unpleasant combination.

"Jesus. Did he *kick* you?"

I don't answer.

"Holy crap," Lex says. "That's low."

"*I* kicked him."

I hear the crunch of pine needles as Lex sits back on his heels. "What?"

"I kicked him," Jordan repeats. She sounds drunk, sort of shrill. "He was *killing* that guy."

"Yeah, right."

"He was! He had his hands around his neck. He couldn't *breathe*."

"Just shut up!" Lex explodes. "He was trying to protect *you,* by the way. If you hadn't been slutty enough to go off with Penn in the first place—"

"I didn't go off with Penn!"

"Then what were you doing out here with him?"

"I don't know what *he* was doing. I went for a walk. I was . . . upset about something."

"Yeah, what?"

"None of your business!"

"Don't flatter yourself, love. Like I care."

"You're an idiot," she spits.

"I'm an idiot? You're the one standing around arguing with me over nothing. And you're the one who fucking *kicked Win in the face*!"

"I told you!" Jordan screams. "I had to!"

"Whatever."

"Is he okay?" Jordan's voice sounds closer, but I've closed both eyes again. I can't see a thing.

"Oh, now you care?"

"Yes. Like you're one to talk. You're a jerk to him every chance you get."

"You don't know anything," Lex says. "You don't."

I flip onto my belly and push to my hands and knees. The entire left side of my face throbs and the tightness I feel must be swelling, but when I blink and squint, I can see. Jordan's boot tip landed on the side of my eye, and while my cheek might be fractured, my vision is fine.

There's a momentary weight lifted, a tiny sense of relief. I am not blind. I breathe deeply but cannot relax. I catch sight of the moon in the far corner of the night sky. It's dipping behind the mountain. It won't be long before it's gone, before the day returns. I shake my head with sudden clarity. It's now or never. It's time to stop wishing, to stop dreaming, to stop waiting.

I crawl forward through tree litter. Sap and rocks stick to

my palms. Lex and Jordan do not look at me. They continue to argue, their voices contentious and heated. Moving hurts. I'm bruised in places other than my face. I haul myself to my feet with a groan. I place one hand on the cliff wall to keep from falling. With my other hand, I begin to unbutton my shirt.

"Winston!" hisses Lex. "Are you okay?"

The shirt falls to the ground. Still leaning against the rock, I use the toe of one shoe to wedge off the other. I have to reach down to remove the second shoe. The socks come next.

"Win!"

I begin walking, sliding my pants down my hips and thighs while I do so. The crisp bite of the night surrounds me. My boxers come off last.

"Seriously, what the fuck," Lex calls after me. "Win, why are your clothes off?"

I keep walking.

"You've got one bony ass, you know."

I walk faster.

They follow. The wind carries their voices.

"What's he on?" Jordan says.

"I don't . . . nothing. Win doesn't do drugs. Ever. He won't even take medicine for his damn motion sickness because he doesn't like things that mess with his head. Guy's a total lightweight. I mean, he had, like, one shot of whiskey tonight and fucking yakked everywhere."

"I thought he didn't drink."

"Yeah, well, good point. But I don't think he's on anything. Seriously."

"Maybe someone slipped him something."

My pulse skyrockets. I struggle not to lose myself in a rising swell of panic.

Lex grunts. "Is your name someone? Because he hasn't been with anyone but me and you tonight, love."

"Where's he going?"

"I don't know. But we can't just let him go off alone. He might . . ."

"Might what?"

"He's got issues, okay? He shouldn't be alone tonight."

"What kind of issues?"

"Forget it. It's none of your business. Just go. I can take care of it."

"You mean like he's going to hurt himself?"

"I didn't say that."

"Yes, you did. Earlier, you said he was a danger to himself and others."

"That was an exaggeration. I was just screwing around."

"Really? He's already been a danger to others. I told you he would have killed Penn. I'm serious."

"Look, I'm serious when I say it's none of your business. I'm sure you're trying to be nice or nurturing or something, but you don't know Win like I do. So why don't you just go on back to the party. Drink some more. Make out with Penn Riggsdale and his friends. And forget all about Winston Winters."

"No way," Jordan snarls.

I do my best to tune them out. Their arguing is irrelevant. It is white noise. I do not want or need them. My wolf is in me, so close, and what I need to do now is chase my own destiny. This much is clear.

I break into a run.

I am driven.

I no longer believe it's up to the moon to tell me what to do.

chapter twenty-eight

antimatter

I wouldn't give Keith the satisfaction of making me cry. I let him haul me by one arm back up to the main road that led toward our grandparents' cabin. People walking downhill to the lake from the parking lot took one look at the mess and stench that was me and skirted to the far side of the trail, their faces pulled back in disgust.

"Why can't I trust you to be, like, at least semi-responsible every now and then?" His black flip-flops slapped on the pavement in a way that didn't appear to fully satisfy his anger. He stomped harder.

"You're acting like I'm a baby!"

"No. You're acting *like* a baby. It's really annoying."

"Let go of me." I wrenched free from his grasp. Keith sort of lunged for me, but I jumped forward and walked a few steps ahead of him. I stayed just out of reach. My long legs stomped along in time with his.

"Dad's going to be pissed," he warned.

"I don't care!"

"You should."

"Why'd Charlie say you were mad at her?" I asked.

I glanced over my shoulder. Keith's stride faltered. He frowned and looked away. He didn't just look mad. He looked embarrassed.

"She was talking to boys, you know," I said, watching to see if this upset him the way I hoped it would. "They were in a boat. They . . . they liked her, I think. Anna, too."

"What boys?"

"Older ones. Like older teenagers. From the campground, I think. They were talking about *sex*."

"Trash," muttered Keith. "All of them."

"What?"

"Never mind. I don't care what Charlie does."

That was disappointing. We crested the driveway of the cabin. My father and grandfather sat on the back porch, drinking something amber out of glasses. Whiskey, probably, but I didn't want to stick around to find out.

As I drew closer, I saw that my grandfather had fallen asleep. A familiar sight: glass still clutched in his hand like his life depended on it, head thrown back in his Adirondack chair, loud snores ringing from his throat and nose. My father had mirrored sunglasses on. But I knew *he* wasn't asleep because he smiled when I first came into view. Then he grimaced at the sight of my clothes.

"What happened?"

Keith trotted up, grim-faced and puffing. "He got on Grand-pa's boat is what happened."

"Ah," my dad said, tipping more of his drink into his mouth. His nose and cheeks were very red.

"Idiot," Keith snarled in my direction.

"Hey, hey. Take it easy on him. He got sick to his stomach. Yelling at him isn't going to make him feel better."

"I'm not trying to make him feel better."

"Oh, really?"

"Dad, he *knows* not to get onto boats!"

"Enough, Keith. Really. I don't want to hear about it. You go hose that deck down, got it?"

My brother folded his arms tightly. Shot daggers in my direction. "Yeah, I got it."

I sidled closer to my dad until Keith looked like he was the one who was going to throw up.

"I'd better get back down there," he mumbled.

"Guess so," my dad said cheerily. When Keith had gone, he wrinkled his nose and inspected me. "Go clean yourself up, Drew."

That evening, my father stationed himself in front of the smoking grill. Another transformation: the genius professor turned typical suburban patriarch. He held a pair of metal tongs in one hand, a glass of liquor in the other, and wore a bright red apron with an illustration of a lobster on the front. Everywhere, our family teemed. Anna and Charlie flipped their hair and took pictures of each other in front of a pine tree. Phoebe drank an energy drink from a can and tried to get Keith to help her with a Sudoku puzzle. My aunt and grandmother labored in the kitchen.

But I kept my eyes on my father. I watched him from the back steps of the porch while swatting mosquitoes from my thighs.

The scent of charring (free-range) chicken fat made my mouth water, and when my uncle slipped inside to get more meat, I went to stand by my father's side in the dwindling summer light.

He tousled my hair.

I shuddered.

He stared down his nose at me. There was no expression on his smooth face. At least none that I understood.

"You're a very intense person," he said.

I didn't take my eyes off him. I longed to hear admiration in his words. Pride.

But I didn't. Under the weight of his gaze, I felt the way I always did, like the weak pup he wished he'd culled. The one he should've tied to a stone and tossed into the ocean.

"I know," I whispered.

"It's hard to watch sometimes." He lapped at the amber drops hanging from the edge of his glass.

"I know," I said again, and I pulled myself up as tall as I could, throwing my shoulders back in the same way he did. Maybe I could get him to look beyond the bandaged neck, the lingering smell of vomit. Maybe I could make him remember my triumphs. Maybe I could make him see me as strong, like him. Not weak, like Keith.

It worked.

He threw an arm around me and pulled me close until I smelled the booze on his breath. "I love you, Drew."

My heart jolted, from the touch and the words. "I love you, too, Dad."

I didn't leave my father's side the rest of the evening. We ate outside, on the side porch, and he let me sit right beside him, very close. The sun slipped away and the night shifted to cool. I held on to his body heat while I bolted down my food.

A screen kept the mosquitoes out, but the chirruping of

crickets and call of a barn owl floated around us. We were a large group, ten people. I stayed very quiet, and I tried to take it all in. Uncle Kirby drank until his eyes turned shiny, and his laugh boomed loud and frightening. Phoebe and her mom sat on either side of him, a matched pair of wide-eyed bookends. Across the table, Anna talked to Grandpa. Dark hair fell across her face, so that I couldn't see her lips moving. When she reached out and poured herself wine, no one said a thing. My father chatted quietly with his mother, who was seated on his left. I could hear their words, very mild ideas, thoughts about my father's research and what he hoped to accomplish. Academic politics. That type of thing. My grandmother, who always spoke her mind, never once mentioned whatever had happened in New York. Or my mother. Or me. That left Keith and Charlie. They sat at the far end of the table. Charlie wore a dress with no sleeves. Her arms were lined with an abundance of silver bracelets. She played with them incessantly, spinning them around and around the slim bones of her wrist. Keith refused to eat. He stared at his food with his head and shoulders down. His eyes looked puffy. A portrait of sheer misery.

I finished everything on my plate. Guzzled down the glass of milk my father set in front of me.

Keith kicked his chair back and stalked from the room without a word.

"Moody one, isn't he?" my aunt said.

"It's the age," her husband said knowingly.

Charlie laughed. Phoebe caught my eye, then looked away. Anna poured more wine.

"He's become a vegetarian," my grandfather announced as if this information might somehow be relevant.

My grandmother brought dessert in. Pound cake and blueberries. I licked whipped cream from my fingers. Belly full, I sat back in my chair. My head began to swim. My eyes began to droop.

When the moon rose halfway into the night sky and the stars twinkled, my father squeezed my shoulder.

"Let's go," he said.

I nodded and followed him silently up to his bedroom on the second floor, forcing my limbs to move. He closed the door and locked it. I sat on the edge of a slippery armchair. It held the greasy scent of pigskin leather. A four-poster bed sat on the other side of the room, beside a wide window of divided light that looked down onto the dark ravine. I yawned.

My father began to undress. The only light came from a bedside lamp, a cast-iron thing in the shape of a candle flame. Its glow was dim, weak.

I turned my head toward the door. The weight of the surrounding darkness flooded over me. I leaned to one side and slid from the chair onto the floor with a crash. My father knelt beside me.

"Drew?"

I couldn't see anything. Just blackness.

He slapped my cheeks. Felt my pulse.

"Drew! Open your eyes."

Open my eyes? I hadn't realized they were closed. I blinked and saw my father's floating face. His long nose and sharp angles. He scooped me up and placed me, not back in the chair, but on his bed, propped against the headboard. Slumped in his arms, I got a whiff of Scotch and sweat, very sour, and my heart raced. Why were all his clothes off? His chest was covered in fur. Like a pelt.

"Dad?"

"What?"

"Where's Siobhan?"

"At home. With your mother. They couldn't make it up here—"

"No! Tonight. Where's Siobhan tonight? Is she safe?"

The creases around his eyes were like slot canyons in the desert. Deep. Impenetrable.

"Siobhan is safe. Okay? Don't worry. Just so long as you relax."

I nodded. The buzzing in my ears began, that soft, chemical calling. A familiar sound. A familiar exiting of my body. A familiar distortion of time and place. My mind sloshed from truth to falsehood. Soon I was not Drew. I was not me.

Soon my clothes were off, too.

Part of me didn't know why.

But a part of me did.

My father stood and walked to the window. He stared out at the full moon. His hands pressed against the glass, long, shadowy fingers splayed like spider legs stuck in a web of leaded panes.

My head bobbed, drugged and heavy.

Don't go to sleep. You'll miss the wolves.

A rattling staccato broke my daze. My eyes widened. The noise originated from my father's fingers as they quivered and rattled against the glass. The sound grew louder, rhythmic and hypnotic. The muscles in his hands tensed until his palms shook, then his arms. Then his whole body.

My mouth worked to call to him, but no sound came out. Instead, I bit down hard on my own fist.

Claws grew from my father's hands like blades of grass sprouting from the earth, and the rattling grew louder, louder. It rose and swelled into an agonizing screech-scratching that made me want to run-flee-hide. I bit down harder

(it'll be over soon)

and the sharp taste of blood filled my mouth. I knew what was happening. I knew what was coming. But I couldn't stop it. I couldn't tear my gaze away. I couldn't help but watch as

(soon soon soon)

he changed.

My father took a step back. His spine bulged and twisted. His skin stretched impossibly in all directions, as if something bad were lodged deep inside him, needing to work its way out. His hands flew to the top of his head, the new blade-claws digging, peeling, rending back his own scalp, a wrinkled gathered mass of hair and flesh that he worked furiously down toward his neck and shoulders.

Hand still jammed in my mouth, I had no more restraint. I screamed.

He twisted in my direction. My father was gone. A black wet whiskered snout pushed from where his head had been. Two dark ears stuck up like bat wings.

I choked. I wanted to die. Maybe I was already dead.

Jaws open wide, the wolf leapt for me.

And the stars began to sing.

Don't look. Don't. Look at the moon instead. Listen to it.

I jerked my head so that I could see out the window, out at the blackest night and the fullest moon. I tried losing myself in the lunar warmth, letting it wash over me, while somewhere else, in another world, another body, another mind, my heart beat madly, madly, too fast, like it wanted its job to just be done, finished, terminated. Over.

This is love, the stars sang. *This is power. This is family.*

Something famished and sick tore at my skin, tore at me. I cried out.

I felt pain. And fear.

But I held tight to the fierce promise of the moon.

I am not broken.

I am savage.

I endured.

chapter
twenty-nine

matter

I chase the night and it's so obvious.

Me. It's been up to me all this time.

What took so long? Deep down I know I may not be as strong as I appear. All these minutes, hours, days, years, spent with Jordan, Lex, Teddy, Mr. Byles, the ballerina, whomever, all this time I've just been stalling. I've clung to the belief that change will come by waiting for it.

How could I have been so stupid?

I aced chemistry. I know how change comes about.

Reactants are transformed into products when the matter involved undergoes an alteration of bonds.

But chemical reactions can take time, a lot of time if there isn't a catalyst to speed things up.

A catalyst.

It's the moon. I need as much of it as possible. In every cell. Every molecule. Every atom. Every quark. I know that now. I can no longer stand in my own way. It's who I am. It's *what* I am. From the kinky coils of my DNA to deeper still, I'm the product of the parts of me that matter and the parts I so wish didn't.

Nothing more.

My bare feet read the forest floor like Braille. I'm heading up the mountain, to the highest elevation possible. The sharp rocks gouging the soles of my feet and the sound of dripping water echoing across the barren talus slopes tell me I'm getting close. I wind higher as the footpath narrows, and as I come around the northern side of the summit trail, rising above the tree line, there's moonlight bouncing off the nearby rock wall, illuminating great sheets of mineral deposits. Sparks of quartz and mica dance in the amber glow, but it's a strain to see real shapes or the trail's sudden drop-off. I grit my teeth and slow down. I can move only so quickly given the darkness and the fact that I'm completely naked.

I bite back a laugh. So much for modesty. Just one more thing I need to let go of.

I think back to that night with Lex. That might have been the closest I've ever gotten to just being me. My true nature. No pretending to be good. No hiding behind different names, behind self-restraint.

A late storm brought snow to Vermont in mid-April. Soft flakes covered newborn crocuses peeking through the wet earth, like the quiet falling of the softest death. Lex wanted me to go with him and Teddy up to Eden for the Rite of Spring

and I told him no like I always did, begging off easily due to a
tennis match the following day. That wasn't the real reason,
though. Crowds made me unhappy. Other people made me unhappy. The way they pulled and pried with their hammer-claw
questions. I had too much to hide to risk putting any part of
myself out into the open. By being vulnerable.

Lex went. I stayed in and studied.

Eventually I grew bored and left our room, with its cramped
corners and stray pieces of Lex's drum equipment scattered
about like fossils. I dragged my feet down from the third floor,
descending to earth slowly, slowly. The halls hummed with
fluorescent lighting, but the dorm was ghost-ship still, every
space abandoned pre-curfew on a Friday night. No one lin-
gered in the common room with the television on or out in the
hall with the stereo up too loud. I was alone. I was friendless. I
slipped into the icy spring night and stole through campus. A
glance into the student lounge told me the freshmen were having hot chocolate and warm cookies. I could have gone in, but
the thought of eating made me uncomfortable because I'd recently started abstaining from food whenever I got too tense or
had too many nightmares. Not eating felt less risky than some
of the other things that came to mind, only now, when I did get
hungry, I felt burdened by this latent weight of guilt. And the
easiest way to avoid the guilt was to not eat some more. Kind
of a lose-lose cycle, but not without its thrills—I'd blacked out
once in film class. After, Lex covered for me and said I had the
flu, which wasn't far from the truth. These days I felt wildly
delirious.

I stuck my hands into the pockets of my jeans and walked
around and around the campus, then into town, where everything was already closed. On my way back, I saw a group of
girls, including the ballerina, sitting on the steps to their dorm,
watching the flurries come down. Despite the cold, the girls

were in their pajamas, done up in pinks and pastels and glittery lip gloss. They laid their heads in each other's laps and played with each other's hair. I held my breath and my chest tightened. Everything about them was unimaginable, untouchable. They laughed and waved to me and said happy last snow. Part of me wanted to stop and talk, but I didn't trust myself. The pressure inside was too much. Self-preservation won out. I simply skulked in the shadows, then headed back to the dorms long before our midnight curfew.

Being back in my room meant more dark thoughts. I turned on Lex's computer to watch some of his porn, but even that didn't offer any relief or release. Seeing all that thrusting and sweating just brought on a gloomy sense of panic and a dull ache in my gut. I shut it off before I finished. Zipped my pants back up. Switched on a local jazz station instead.

There was a soft knock on the door. Against my better judgment, I turned the handle and found myself looking into the wide doe eyes of the ballerina's roommate. Lex's girl. She stood there, a true vision, almost achingly lovely with thick black hair that spilled down her back in shiny waves and a smattering of brown freckles that splashed across the warm glow of her skin.

"Can I wait here?" she asked, her voice husky and low. "You know, for Lex?"

I gave her a hard look. "Lex is gone."

"He'll be back." She walked in tentatively, brushing against me. She smelled of smoke and peaches. "God, your side is clean," she said, looking around. She moved toward my bookshelf and ran her fingers horizontally across the spines.

I followed.

"Your walls." She gestured.

"What?" I asked.

"There's nothing on them." This was true. A number of syllabi and study guides were pinned to a bulletin board that hung adjacent to my desk, but other than that, the only item I'd put up was a small, framed photo of a brown-and-white collie. A long-dead friend. The girl studied it briefly but didn't comment.

"Well, make yourself at home." I lay down on my bed.

The girl said nothing.

I closed my eyes.

The radiator hissed and gurgled. John Lee Hooker strummed his guitar and sang sadly. The trees outside whipped violently in a sudden wind. Snow continued to fall. We were quiet for a long time.

"I love this book," she said suddenly. I opened an eye and saw her sitting on the floor, holding my worn copy of *The Chocolate War*.

"You've read it?"

"Don't sound so surprised."

I shrugged and put my arms behind my head.

"You think a girl like me doesn't read?"

I smiled.

Five more minutes passed.

"What kind of name is Winston?"

"Excuse me?"

"Is that your first name? Or your last name?"

"I wasn't aware we were on a first-name basis."

More silence.

"Winston is my father's name," I offered after a moment.

"Oh, yeah? What's he like, your dad?"

"He's an economics professor. Or, he used to be."

"He sounds smart," she said.

"I don't know about that."

"Like father, like son."

I didn't answer.

The girl got on her hands and knees. She crawled toward me.

"So, is it true?" she whispered.

"Is what true?" I whispered back.

"That you . . . that you're as crazy as Lex says. He says you're, like, anorexic. Or something."

I rolled onto my side and looked her in the eye. "Oh, well, if Lex told you that, then it must be true."

A flash of confusion crossed her face, but she recovered. She sat up and wound a lock of inky hair around her index finger.

"I'm not trying to be nosy, you know. Everyone's a little bit crazy, right? I just thought it was interesting. Guys don't usually—"

I cut her off with a dark look.

She laughed nervously. "You're funny."

"Am I?"

The girl nodded. She inched even closer and put her hand on the bed next to mine so that our fingers were almost touching. Then she breathed deeply, the round swell of her breasts lifting on inhalation, and I knew what was coming.

I knew what she was going to do.

I simply closed my eyes and waited for her soft lips to touch mine.

Lex saw her leaving as he came back. I don't know what she said or what she didn't. But he knew. I could tell from the moment he slammed the door shut. From the snow melting in his hair and the tears melting on his cheeks. From the way he wouldn't meet my gaze.

I lay belly-down on my bed, reading Robert Cormier.

"Well, now I know why you didn't want to come." His words slurred together. "Too bad the party got snowed out, huh?"

I said nothing.

"Asshole move, Win."

Still I said nothing.

"Did you fuck her?"

"No."

He swiped at his eyes. "All I've done is *kiss* her."

"Well, it's not like I forced her," I said. I rolled over and stared at the ceiling. A water stain in the shape of Japan stretched from the far corner above me.

"I don't get it. I thought you were a virgin, man. Like totally inexperienced. You won't even touch Brynn's tits, but you'll let the girl I like do *that* to you?"

My head felt very dark. Black. I had no answer for what he was asking. He didn't want to know. I never said I was a virgin.

"She said you knew what you were doing. You told her what to do."

"You have to take charge with girls. Tell them what you want."

"What's *wrong* with you?" he whispered.

"I'm not a good person."

"No shit."

"I mean it."

Lex lurched across the room toward me, eyes bloodshot and wild. He lost his footing on the slick covers of his own rock magazines and went down hard on his side with an *oof*. He tried but couldn't get himself up again. Still on his knees, he raised one arm and pointed at me. "I. Hate. Excuses."

"I don't have one," I said.

"Then why'd you do it?"

"Oh, so now you *want* an excuse?"

"I want to know *why!*"

"I told you," I said. "There's nothing good about me. Nothing at all. I—"

"Shut up."

I shut up.

He sat back. Shook his head vigorously like he had water stuck in his ear. "Why did you say that?"

"Because it's true."

"God, I hate you!" Lex turned and crawled toward his bed. He hauled one arm onto the twin mattress and put his head down. It sounded like he was sobbing.

My heart pounded. I had lots of thoughts, too many. I thought, *Go to him*. I thought, *Apologize, make a joke, say something, say anything*. I thought, *That's what a real friend would do*.

I did none of those things.

I rolled over and went to sleep.

I have good instincts. Very good instincts. It still took a minute to register that Lex wasn't in the same place when I woke up. He lay on the floor, but not in front of his bed where I'd last seen him. Instead he was slouched beside my desk, face slack, arms splayed. My nose wrinkled. It smelled like he'd gotten sick. I didn't want to know where. My alarm clock flashed 3:15. In the morning. The world around me was black. And silent. Utterly silent. What had woken me up?

I swung my feet to the floor. My heart leapt into my throat when I saw that Lex had touched my desk. For a second, I thought he'd found my photo album. The one I kept hidden in the bottom drawer. Besides the pictures of my family, I had other things in there—like clippings from the newspapers and the magazines. Like my brother's and sister's obituaries and all those articles about *me*. With my face. My real name. But as I got closer to Lex, I saw I was mistaken. Snow layered my desk, not memories. He'd opened the window before passing out.

He'd let in winter's end.

They wouldn't let me ride with him in the ambulance, but I raised hell to drive over to the medical center with Mr.

Galveston, our dorm parent, after I called 911. The ER physician and the police asked me a lot of questions. What he'd taken. When. Why. With whom. Had I seen him at all? My legs shook and I answered as obliquely as I could. I knew nothing.

I crept into the hospital room hours later. Lex might be angry with me, but he was alone and I couldn't just abandon him. His parents were three thousand miles away. Who else would visit him? I sat by his bed. I saw the bruises on his face, the IV in his arm. I hated myself.

His eyes fluttered open, very blue. He saw me. He couldn't talk.

"They pumped your stomach," I told him. "But you're going to be okay."

He blinked.

"I told them you drank too much. That it was an accident. You didn't know your limit."

He wheezed.

I hunched forward in my chair. "Look, I haven't been honest with you, Lex. What I said earlier, about being a bad person, it's true. There's a reason I don't talk about my family and it doesn't have anything to do with my parents' divorce or me not getting along with my mom. It has to do with *me*. Who I really am. My real name. It's not Winston. . . ."

I kept talking. The two words I intended to say, *I'm sorry,* wouldn't come. But other words did, ones I'd never given voice to. I struggled to say them. Lex struggled to listen. As I continued talking, he looked away. Maybe he didn't believe me. Maybe he didn't want to hear what I had to say. My wretched guilt. But sitting in that room, in the weak light of morning, for the first time since their deaths, I couldn't stop talking. I told him everything.

About Keith and Siobhan.

About how they'd died and who I was and what I'd done.
About what it all meant.
About what I would become.
What I *had* to become.
My destiny.

chapter
thirty

antimatter

I heard voices on the front porch.

Whispers. What sounded like crying. Or laughter.

My body refused to move.

"Just shut up!" a female voice rang out.

More mumbling.

"No. Just go, okay? Go!"

I finally sat up. Looked around. I was on the couch in the living room of my grandfather's cabin, and I was in shock.

Some part of me hurt. Badly. A type of pain and a type of place I didn't have words for. My head lolled, heavy with a funny residue that reminded me of Phenergan or worse. Only I hadn't traveled anywhere. Had I? I tried to remember. I'd gone upstairs with my dad. I had seen a wolf. So why was I down here, all alone, in the living room, with just a—

Sssnap!

I whimpered.

No. That didn't happen. No one hurt you. Not like that. Push it away. Remember the wolves instead.

The door slammed shut. Footsteps approached.

I waited. Anna appeared in the threshold. Her head turned and she saw me. Her legs buckled and she almost fell. Then she laughed, a wild, out-of-control sound, and put a finger to her lips.

"Shhh," she said. "You're not supposed to be up. It's too late for you."

I bit the inside of my cheek.

Anna came closer, crossing the floor with a looping twist of her feet. Her hair was very messy and she smelled different, pungent, almost smoky. I couldn't place it. I had a large fleece blanket wrapped around me but still couldn't remember how I had gotten here. I didn't think I wanted to remember. A part of me wanted to cry. Or scream.

Anna leaned against the back of the couch, then swung her long legs over to sit beside me. She peeled off her jacket. She had nothing on beneath it.

I blinked. I had to still be dreaming. I had to be. None of this, my confusion, my fear, my bubbling well of insanity, the half-naked girl in front of me, it couldn't be real.

The roar of a car engine filled the room. Headlights flashed through the window, cutting across Anna's face.

"Shh," she said again. "This is our secret, little Drew. Okay? Don't be scared."

Sssnap!

Another flash. This one too vivid. Too real.

I gagged.

Anna's dark eyes narrowed. "What's wrong?"

I couldn't answer.

"Could you hear what Ricky and I were saying outside?"

I still couldn't answer.

Anna leaned forward to grab on to me, filling my head with her bad smoke-smell. I reared back with a tiny growl and my heart beat hummingbird fast. I didn't want to be touched.

I didn't want to be touched.

She babbled, "Look, it was an accident. I swear. Please, Drew, just don't freak out, all right? You can't tell anyone, you just can't. Ricky was drinking, well, I was, too, and it just happened so *fast*. I mean, he came out of nowhere! But it was a total accident, I swear, Drew. I swear. We tried to help him, we both did, but we couldn't do *anything*. I told Ricky that we're both leaving soon, we need to forget this ever happened. He's back at Colgate in the fall and I'm going to be a senior this year. We can't just, like, ruin *everything* over an accident, right? You get that? You understand?"

I had no idea what she was talking about, I didn't want to know, but she reached for me again, pleading and desperate.

I hit her.

Anna gave a yelp and her whole arm tensed. Like she meant to hit me back.

I kicked her in the stomach.

She froze, her face sliding into a mask of pain and disbelief. Then she fell back against the couch cushions and began to cry, coarse, jagged sobs. I stared. Anna's tears evoked nothing in me. I did not care.

I continued to stare at her, at her body. Like yesterday morning, small sticks and dry leaves lay tangled in her hair. But unlike yesterday, dark spots were now crusted across her cheeks, her hands, her forearms. Crimson and brown. Blood.

The sobbing ceased. She turned her face sideways and

watched me, too. Her side heaved with each breath, and her one visible eye drooped with fatigue. The lid began to close. I crept forward from where I lay huddled until I was on my hands and knees. I inched forward even more, crawling over her with my arms anchored on each side of her torso. I liked the way my shadow fell across her bare body. I used one hand to push her onto her back. I wanted to take her in. She grunted and strained to lean forward. I pushed her back again. And again. There was nothing sleepy in her expression anymore, but she finally lay still, tolerating me as a bitch would her whelp. Anna's nipples were very pink and I saw a small line of moles running down her stomach. I reached out and touched one of her breasts. I'd never felt anything like it before. It was warm, very soft, with real weight to it.

The pounding of my head made me unsteady. I sat back and winced. *Whoosh.* It felt like the wind had been knocked out of me. All at once. Colored dots danced before my eyes. I thought I might faint.

Something in my breathing alarmed Anna. Before I knew what was happening, she moved right beside me, gripping me tightly. She was very strong. I didn't fight her this time. I couldn't. I crumpled in her arms and my face felt wet. I ran a hand beneath my nose. Ribbons of snot flew everywhere. Was I crying, too?

"Anna," I squeaked. "Anna, I—"

"Hush," she said, and a sour waft of her breath came at me, like something familiar and recent. She held me close.

The slurred words she panted in my ear were familiar, too.

"It's okay, Drew. I promise. This, tonight, we'll just keep everything between us, all right? I know you like me. You don't want to get me in trouble. So you and I, let's both forget that any of this ever happened."

chapter
thirty-one

matter

I've reached the highest point I can. I'm at the peak, a craggy cliff that looks down onto the smoldering bonfire and smoldering party and out over the woods, toward the sleeping school, the sleeping town, the sleeping state.

I stand on all fours. I open my throat to howl.

Nothing comes out.

I try again. I consciously will my body to give rise to my voice. To let me sing with every need, every desire, every lament that writhes and simmers within my molecules, every bond that holds me together and every action that tears me apart.

No howl. Instead I hear breathing, my own. And I hear the scrabbling and fear in the steps and voices of the two who have followed me. I don't get why they're here. I want them to leave. If I change, I won't know who they are. I won't be able to discriminate their goodness from my badness.

I will hurt them.

"A w-wolf?" I hear Jordan say from the shadows beneath me, at the base of the rock, and I know Lex has told her what I shared with him last spring in that miserable hospital room. We never talked about it after that. Lex was put on probation and moved to a freshman dorm, where the rules were stricter. I was left alone.

"What docs that mean?" she asks.

"Well, hmm, given the current situation, it means he's really fucked up. He thinks . . . he thinks he's going to change into one."

"He really believes that?"

"Well, what the hell do you think? That he's just up there naked on that rock for shits and giggles?"

"No, I, I, it's just so . . ."

"So what?"

"It's so sad."

Lex makes a funny sound. Like he's being strangled.

"We should help him," Jordan says. "Get help for him."

"No way."

"Why not?"

"That's his choice. To get help. You can't force somebody to do that."

"What if he hurts himself?"

"We can't stop him."

"What if he hurts someone else?"

"He won't."

"He already has," she insists.

"That was dumb. I told you, he thought Penn was going to rape you or something. And maybe he was. He was coming after you, you know."

"Has Win gotten into fights before?"

There's a long pause. I'm sure Lex is thinking about how I attacked him in the biology lab.

"Just once," he says. "That I know of."

"When?"

"Last year."

My knees quake. Of course I know what he's talking about. It's just so not what I expected him to say. He wasn't there.

Lex speaks: "You know Win plays tennis, right? He's like a prep legend."

"He told me he doesn't play anymore."

"He really said that?"

"Yup."

"Crazy," Lex mutters, sounding stunned.

"What happened?" Jordan asks.

"He beat the crap out of the assistant coach."

"He did?"

"Yup. Broke his wrist, I think. Maybe a rib, too. Guy didn't come back after that. I didn't see it, but everyone said that one minute they were just talking to each other and the next Win went after him. No warning or anything."

"Wouldn't that get him kicked out of school?"

"No. I told you. He's like a god when it comes to tennis. He never loses. Never. And so no one gives a fuck what Win Winters does."

I shift my weight around. That's not really true. A lot of people give a fuck. But it was right after the deal with Lex, and when I told the headmaster what the coach had said to me, he understood why I'd been mad. He understood why I couldn't control my anger.

So it was your roommate this time, Winters? I know who you are. You're not fooling me. You're like the touch of death, aren't you? There's something about you that just makes people wish they were dead. . . .

"Lex," Jordan starts.

"I'm not snitching on him, so shut up about that. You can do what you want, but I'm going to stay here and be with him. He'll be different when the sun comes up. I know he will. I'll be able to talk to him then."

"I'll stay with you," she says quickly.

"Why? You don't have to."

"I will. I'm not leaving you guys here. It's like two hours until morning, right?"

Two hours. Urgency and longing pulse through me. I lift my head higher. I try to howl one more time.

Nothing.

I lay my chest against the rock.

I wait.

chapter
thirty-two

antimatter

I returned to Charlottesville at the end of the summer. Two months later, I won our club's Fall Classic tourney with ease. My parents cheered for me. Everyone did. I had no competition. I was peerless.

That same year, Keith withered while I flourished.

High school stole his confidence. His friends. His happiness. He spent days in bed, not talking, not eating. Just sleeping or staring at the ceiling.

Lee came over a couple of times, but Keith would lock his door and turn his music up very loud. He kept listening to that depressing Australian band and their song about thieving birds over and over. I hated it.

"Get out of here," Lee said to me one afternoon. He'd caught me spying on him from the back stairwell.

"You're fat," I replied.

"Is that supposed to be an insult?"

"Well, you are."

"Yeah, big fucking deal. You think this is my first time at the fat boy rodeo? If you want to hurt me, you're gonna have to try harder, kid."

"Leave Keith alone. He doesn't want to talk to you."

Lee walked down the hall toward me. He had khaki-colored parachute pants on and they made a swishing sound when he moved.

"You need to stay out of things that aren't any of your business," he snapped.

"My brother is my business."

"God, you're a pinhead. Don't you get it? I actually care about him. He's going to fail out of school if I don't help him."

"I'll kill you," I said, arching my back and creeping forward on my hands and knees. I curled my fingernails into the hardwood floor deep enough to leave marks. "If you don't leave him alone, I'll rip your head off. I'll cut your fat body into fat little pieces. I'll—"

"Drew!"

We both started. Keith stood in the hallway. His shoulders drooped. His eyes were very red and his cheeks were very hollow.

Lee trotted toward him. Swish, swish, swish, went his pants. They went into his room and closed the door.

I tossed and turned in my bed. Pilot curled at my feet as always.

A soft voice called my name.

I tossed more.

In my mind, the moon was full and I dreamed of wolves. I dreamed of power I would someday have.

"Drew . . ." The voice came again, pulling me into wakefulness.

"Go away," I muttered, waving my arm.

"Can I sleep with you? I had a nightmare."

My eyes fluttered open. Siobhan, sweet Siobhan, stood beside my bed, wearing a flowered nightgown and with her honey hair all rumpled. Her soft face held a flat expression, like she had no feelings, no depth, inside of her.

I sat up. I knew that look. I'd seen it in the mirror myself ever since that dark summer night. Not in New Hampshire, but another night, a year earlier, here, in my very own room. A night when I was not alone and not safe. A night when a monster had first prowled in, too familiar to resist.

A night *before*.

Before I hit Soren.

Before I became *bad*.

"Drew," Siobhan whimpered. "Please. I'm scared."

"Yeah, fine," I mumbled, thinking of all the times Keith had comforted me up in Concord when Pilot wasn't around. The way I'd needed him to feel protected. The bed creaked as my sister crawled beneath the sheets. I rolled onto my side. She curled against me.

"I need to talk to you," I told Keith. My legs trembled.

He sat on the edge of the flagstone patio. The leaves had all fallen. The forecast called for a rare December snow. Something bright and glossy fluttered in his hands.

"What is that?" I asked, pointing.

Keith held it out to me. It was a brochure from the wildlife preserve we'd visited over a year ago. Semper Liberi, the place that kept animals too damaged to live on their own.

"I thought I wanted to work there," he said listlessly. "Some-day."

"But now?"

"Now I don't want to anymore."

"Why not?"

"Because sometimes trying to make a difference is worse than not trying at all."

"Oh."

"What did you want to talk about?"

"Siobhan."

Keith blinked at me. Those coppery eyes.

"What about Siobhan?" he asked.

I told him how she had come to my room. How I let her sleep in my bed. The things she'd tried to do to me. Her hot tears on my back and small hands on my body, all over, *everywhere*, becoming more desperate the more I pulled away. Until I felt like my rejection was hurting her. Until I didn't know what the right thing to do was anymore.

Keith turned very pale. Then he got up and ran inside the house.

Should I not have told him? I followed Keith. I found him locked in the downstairs bathroom. He stayed in there a long time. The noises he made meant he was either really sick or really sad. Or both.

He wouldn't look at me when he came out.

"I'm sorry," was all he said. "I'm so sorry."

chapter
thirty-three

the sea

Jordan climbs up onto the rock first. I don't look, but I know it's her. The clues are there. She's quiet, contained, so different from Lex and his blundering movements. And she must have seen more of my charm than my strangeness tonight, because she's kind. She's gentle. Jordan touches my arm. My back. The bruise around my eye. I let her. It's okay. I'm lying down now, so it's not like she sees too much of me.

My panting increases in her presence. I guess that's why she's touching. She wants me to stay calm. But she keeps saying, *Win, Win,* and that's what makes me shake and pant more. She doesn't know I hate my name, that every time I hear it, I'm reminded of what I've lost. My family. My identity. My innocence.

I'm reminded of *him*.

She keeps talking, a sad little soliloquy. She tells me she's from California and that she doesn't fit in here. She tells me she's never really fit in anywhere, but that the money and elitism at our school intimidates her. She says this embarrasses her in ways she doesn't understand. She tells me about life in California, about public school and kids who ride the bus and who hang out at strip malls or in front of liquor stores. She tells me about doing too many drugs and making too many bad decisions and deciding to come here so that she could be in a place where her past didn't have to define her. She says earning a scholarship made her proud until she got here and realized it was something to be ashamed of. She tells me about her mother and visiting family in Guadalajara at Christmastime. She talks about something called Las Posadas, a Catholic tradition in Mexico where families walk door to door, pretending to be Mary and Joseph looking for a place to stay before Jesus is born. And she sings to me in Spanish, sweet, lilting words I cannot understand. She does not talk about her father.

I don't answer. I can't and I don't want to. The moon is leaving, very quickly, a pale shadow slipping behind the neighboring mountains. Has it taken part of me with it? I haven't changed, and so yes, I think, yes, it has.

Eventually Lex scrambles up, too. He sits on the other side of me. He smells of cigarettes but doesn't light up. He says nothing, which I appreciate.

Together we wait for the sun.

after

We do not say that *possibly* a dog talks to itself. Is that because we are so minutely acquainted with its soul?

—Ludwig Wittgenstein, *Philosophical Investigations*

chapter
thirty-four

half-life

The night is gone.

Extinguished.

Extinct.

The sun is barely visible, but the ripe colors of the sky blossom, bright and welcoming. The memories rip through me, along with that nostalgic pang of mourning, the kind that marks both a beginning and an end. I do not move. I remain on the rock, on my stomach, and I do not move. I can't.

Jordan and Lex both leave the summit. They have to pee, they tell me, which I don't doubt, but they're gone such a long time that I'm pretty sure their motives are multiple.

What do I do? I creep to the edge of the boulder, past the scrub brush and a hive of carpenter ants, almost to the point of no return. I've failed again. I've failed like I've always failed. The disappointment and self-loathing push me ever closer to the drop. Spite makes everything easier, and in this moment I feel like I could do it. I could take this leap of faith that I failed to take all those years ago.

But the wolf won't let me.

Come out, then, I plead with it. *Show yourself. Don't hide.*

I can feel it inside of me. It is feral. Hungry. But it doesn't come out. Instead, the wolf inside me turns around three times, tamping down hope and healing and grace like soft meadow grass. Then it lies down. It tucks its tail. It closes its eyes.

I try. I can't wake it. It's too late.

I scoot back from the edge. Sit on my bare ass. I have to accept the truth in front of my nose. This wasn't my cycle.

My mind clicks ahead, shuttering into the future. Twenty-nine days until the next full moon. What else can I do but wait? This cycle wasn't for naught. I know more. I think I was close. Now I understand the strength of the moon. The need to be near to it, to be naked, to find as much wildness within myself as I can, right down to my most elemental parts. That's where change begins. Power, too. I know that now. I will do this again. I will try harder.

I hear voices. My body starts. I take a quick inventory of the approaching figures. It's just Jordan and Lex. My surprise at their return is tempered only by my relief that they haven't brought anyone else with them. I thought they would.

"Do us a favor," Lex calls. He throws something at me. "Put these on, okay? Sunrise means it's time to cover your junk."

I look at the items on the ground. My boxers and pants. I acquiesce and pick them up. I can fool people, but maintaining distance is key. I think I clung to these two last night because of some inner conflict. Inner resistance. Weakness. It is a mistake I cannot afford to make again.

When I'm dressed, Jordan comes over.

"Sit down," she says.

"Why?"

"I want to tell you something."

Maybe she wants to tell me how worried she is about me. Or ask if I'm okay. I ready myself for her questions. I will say the right things. I will say the things that will make her leave. The things that will make her not care if I live or die. I've done it before.

I can attract, and I can also repel.

As I sit, I glance at Lex. He's about twenty feet away, standing with his back against a small boulder. He's looking at his phone.

Jordan and I face the north. We can see nothing but trees.

"What do you want to tell me?" I ask.

"Last night," she begins, "I wasn't totally honest with you."

"Okay."

"I was drunk."

"Yeah."

"But that's not an excuse, you know? After you left, I was talking with Penn and his friends. They were being total guy jerks, asking me why I dress the way I do, why I haven't figured out how to get guys to like me, and if I'm some kind of angry, man-hating feminazi."

"Sounds like typical Penn."

"So I told him to meet me in the woods. That I'd show him what I know about getting guys to like me."

I stare at her. "You did that? Why?"

Her face is all pinched and her tired eyes burn hot. "Do you have to ask?"

"Yes!"

"Because I was pissed! Because I wanted to be more powerful than him."

"But what were you going to do?"

"I don't know!"

"You don't *know*?"

Jordan folds her arms and leans away from me. "You don't get to judge me. My choices are mine, okay? I just wanted to say thank you. For what you did. You looked out for me. No one's ever done that before."

I blink, confused. I've made her mad and she's *thanking* me?

"Win."

I glance up. Lex stands before me.

"We need to talk."

"Oh, okay." I'm not really listening. I'm still thinking about what Jordan just said. I'm still sort of stunned.

"I mean it." Lex sounds serious. He has one hand on his hip and his phone in the other.

I nod. "You get reception out here? I don't."

He crouches beside me. Slips the phone away. "Stop it, Win. You need to listen to me. Now."

"Sure."

"I'm worried about you. We both are."

I rub my palms on the front of my pants. I feel hot and it's hard to breathe. "D-did you, like, call somebody? About me?"

"Why would I do that?"

"I don't know," I whisper.

Jordan reaches out. She places a hand on my shoulder and pushes down with her warm fingers.

The pressure's too much. I get up and start walking. I think I should go. I think I should get off this mountain.

Lex follows, trotting alongside me. "It's that guy, that dead guy, right? You think you killed him?"

My stride falters. "M-maybe."

"Win, you didn't. Seriously."

"You don't know that."

"I *do*," he insists.

"*I* don't."

Lex grabs my arm, stopping me before I can reach the descending trail. He pulls me toward him.

"Look, I've been here, too," he says roughly. "Okay?"

"Where?"

"Here! Hating myself. Wanting to end it all."

"You have?"

He blushes. "I think you know that."

"I guess."

"I felt helpless then, Win. Hopeless, too. I don't want you to feel that way."

"I'm not going to kill myself."

"But you've tried before. When you were just a *kid*."

"I didn't try," I say.

"Yes, you did. You told me. You were going to jump off that bridge. You had a plan."

A plan.

(*Get up, Drew. We're leaving. I'll tell you why when we get there.*)

"I didn't try," I say again, but I feel myself slipping. Why doesn't he get it? Why doesn't he get that that's the whole point? The whole problem? "I changed my mind."

Lex continues to stare. The look on his face is not easy for me to recognize. It's too serious. Too tense. Behind him, Jordan gets up from where we sat looking out at the trees. She comes toward us, wiping dirt from her hands as she walks. My heart jackhammers. I don't know what they're trying to do. I don't know what they're trying to prove, but I'm uncomfortable. I'm more than uncomfortable.

This is painful.

"You need help," Lex says, and I shake my head. I mean, who could help me? It's not like people haven't tried before.

But what is there to say when what's inside of me is unspeakable?

"You can't do anything," I tell Lex, and it's true. My own mom gave up on me. She's the one who sent me away to boarding school. She's the one who said I needed to be somewhere where people didn't know who I was or what I'd done. I don't think she was wrong about that.

"Yes, we can. We're taking you to a hospital. A psychiatric one. Right now. I know where to go. Okay, Win? Everything will be okay."

Will it?

I find that very hard to believe.

chapter
thirty-five

to the stars

We leave Eden.

 We stumble out of the woods.

 The bridge appears in the distance.

 My past catches up with me.

 Ssssnap!

 The three of us trudge along the edge of the river. My legs hurt and I lag behind the others. I watch as her small fingers dart out to grab at the blooming vines of jasmine that cluster along the roadside. She plucks the white flowers, one-two-three, then crumples them, scattering the ruined petals like bread crumbs.

 Their conversation floats back.

"Why do we have to walk?" she asks, craning her neck to look up at him. "This is taking forever."

"Because he can't ride the bus."

"He can't do anything."

"Shut up," I call out.

She ignores me. "How much farther is it?"

"You ask too many questions."

"That's my job," she replies brightly. "I ask questions. You answer them. Every question has an answer, you know." She circles back to me, worming her fingers into mine, tugging at my hand. I shake her off. She laughs, then grabs for me again, this time snaking her thin arm around my waist. I shiver.

"Stop it," I tell her.

"I love you," she says sweetly. Too sweetly.

"Leave me alone."

She pouts. "You're being mean."

I'm not mean, I think, but then she skips ahead and takes his hand, and my heart flares with something black, like jealousy or ire, and so maybe I am. Mean.

A bridge appears in the distance. A rusted span stretched high above the glassy water.

"Tell me where we're going," she says.

"We're almost there."

"But what'll it be like?"

"It'll be good," he says. "Better than good. Where we're going, we'll never have to grow up and turn into anything we don't want to be."

She thinks about this. "Really?"

"Really. Remember the story of Peter Pan? It'll be just like that."

"You mean, like magic?"

"Just like magic."

She nods solemnly. "I like that."

"Me too."

"What is there to do there?"

"Well, what's your favorite thing in the whole world?"

"Favorite what?"

"Anything?"

"Horses," she says. "Arabian ones. Like the Black Stallion."

"Then that's what'll be waiting for you. Your very own horse."

"Huh?"

"What's your least favorite thing?"

She begins to spin in a circle, slow then fast, long hair streaming out with comet-tail force. Her eyes close, very tight, and her pale face fills with lines, like a tiger's mask.

"Monsters," she whispers.

He glances at the bridge, then back at me. "Then that's what won't be there. No monsters. Ever."

The spinning ceases. "You promise?"

"Yes," he says. "I promise."

chapter
thirty-six

siobhan

I blink.

My eyes sting.

The dawn is too bright.

I sit up and look around. I'm riding in a borrowed car with Lex and Jordan—Teddy's BMW. We're winding down the mountain away from the school. Lex fiddles with the stereo while he drives, and the music that comes on is sort of folksy. Sort of sad. It reminds me that he's from Seattle. Jordan sits beside him in the front. She picks at the buckle of her leather boot. My knees press against the back of her seat. I'm too tall for a coupe.

I'm dazed. I run my hand through my hair. I know where

we're going, but I don't understand how any of this came about. I don't understand why they're doing this for me. They are not my friends. I have gone out of my way to make sure of that.

Getting to Burlington takes over an hour on the interstate, and in Vermont, interstate means a two-lane road. I stare out the window. Lake Champlain sparkles on our left. Great glittering sunrise diamonds dance across its surface as the cool shadows of New York keep watch in the distance.

My head begins to hurt as the road winds and we get stuck behind a truck blowing thick clouds of diesel exhaust everywhere. Jordan realizes what's going on with me, which I'm grateful for because I can't talk, but she reaches back for my hand and holds on to it, which I don't like. She gets Lex to pull over on the side of the road. I kneel in the grass and try really hard not to get sick, but of course I do. Only for the first time no one acts disgusted or scornful.

Jordan and Lex get out of the car with me. I keep my back to them, but I listen to their chatting, their voices full of light and ease. Lex is smoking, and it sounds like Jordan's found his book of matches. He makes a habit of drawing little faces on each individual match with a fine-point pen and relishes watching the tiny red heads go up in flames when he needs his nicotine fix. Jordan calls him a sadist, which he doesn't deny, but she's not bothered by it. I can tell.

I don't rejoin them right away. I let them talk. Maybe it's the cadence and timbre of their speech or the meaning of their words. Maybe it's the way the morning sun cuts the swirling valley mist or the way dew beads across the laces of my shoes, but my heart burns like flames lick ice. I am bound between two worlds. I don't want to die and I don't think I can live. How can the same God that created all this beauty have created me?

A stake of wood and a hanging sign tell me the property I'm crouched on is for sale: two hundred acres of countryside. The house sits far back from the road, and the windows have been boarded up. A weathered barn sways with the breeze, rocking gently on its exposed foundation. Beyond that sit woods. I spy a brown wolf with hungry eyes not ten feet away, wriggling beneath the post-and-rail fence. It struggles, haunches churning, forelegs scrabbling at the earth, and then it's free. The animal drops its head, shakes, then pads into the field without caution. Approaching the tree line, it breaks into a lope, great bounding strides. Its coat shimmers like dripping honey. Then it is gone.

Swallowed up.

Jordan and Lex have their arms around mine. They're pulling me off the fence because I've got one leg over already. They're talking to me, telling me things, but my ears are filled with a desperate keening, a feral moan. They both pull harder. My shirt rips. I flail back and land hard on the ground.

"Shit!" says Jordan, wringing her hands. "I'm sorry."

"Don't do this, Win," Lex says sharply. "Get up."

I think of Siobhan's hair fluttering in the wind as she drops, so fast.

I moan again.

There is no turning back.

Jordan crouches beside me. "Can you get in the car? We're almost there."

I shake my head very quickly. My eyes sting again, making everything blurry. One of them shoves a water bottle into my hand.

"This is bullshit," says Lex, despite a shushing from Jordan. "If I have to call the cops to haul your ass to the hospital, then that means I'll have to dump my stash right here, let the wildlife get high. And I really don't want to do that, Win. Don't make me do that. Let's just go."

"I saw her," I say as I struggle to my feet. I want to look back, past the fence, the meadow. Into the woods. I want to, but I can't. I take a step toward the car.

"Saw who?" Jordan asks.

"My sister."

chapter
thirty-seven

admission

The emergency room is staffed by air traffic controllers. I get the impression everything is communicated through semaphore. Or telepathy. Because besides the occasional page over the intercom, the place is quieter than it should be. A local television show highlighting fall color and apple picking plays out on one screen. On the other is a movie with Denzel Washington. *The Manchurian Candidate*, I think, which is pretty appropriate considering how the people waiting look hypnotized. Jordan is told to stay with me so I don't bolt, but really, what's she going to do if I try? Kick me in the face again? Lex writes my name on an admittance sheet, then comes back with a clipboard and some paperwork. He begins to fill it out on his own.

"Let me do that," I say.

"I'm just filling out the parts I can."

"What does it ask?"

"It asks why you're here, okay? Like the sign-in sheet, only there's more room and more questions. Hey, are you allergic to any medications?"

I sit up. "What did you put?"

"Well, if you don't tell me, I'm going to put 'Don't know.'"

"No. What did you put for why we're here?"

"I put that you're really stressed. That you're, uh, having a hard time."

I snatch the clipboard and look. He's written "mental breakdown" in the Reason for Visit section, and under a list of psychiatric symptoms he's checked boxes for suicidal ideation, homicidal ideation, active hallucinations, delusional thinking, disordered thoughts, agitation, and history of trauma.

"This is all wrong," I mumble, but my hands shake too much and the clipboard falls.

"I'll write," Jordan says, bending to pick it up. "You tell me what to put."

I nod.

She squints at the paper. Scrawls down the date. "What's your middle name, Win?"

I stand and begin to pace.

Lex says, "His middle name is Winston. His first name . . . it's Andrew."

"Andrew Winston Winters," Jordan says, and when Lex tells her I'm from Charlottesville, I know she's put the pieces together. It's been almost six years, but people still know my name. It's hard to forget. When it happened, the whole thing was all over the news: television, magazines, social media, all of it, highlighted as a failure of our culture, a symptom of a larger disease. Everyone, over and over again, asking the same question, the one I'd never, ever answered: Why? Why would three *children* have a suicide pact?

And why would one back out and let the other two die?

Lex clears his throat. "You know, you're going to have to call your parents."

Hours later, my name gets called.

I tell the ER nurse who interviews me that I have a wolf inside of me and I can't get him to come out. She smiles and nods and listens to my heart. Then she takes my blood and my blood pressure, makes me piss in a cup. She also gives me an ice pack for my hurt eye and has a tech sit with me. There's more waiting. A doctor comes in next. He asks even more questions. I do my best to answer them. I try explaining about the wolf and how I don't *want* to hurt anyone even though I might not be able to help it, but after a certain point, my vocal cords won't make words.

Only howls.

I want ice for all my wounds.

The doctor's voice turns solemn. He explains that he's going to admit me into the hospital's adolescent psych unit for evaluation. I nod when he asks if I understand. Then I'm allowed to say good-byes and thank-yous to Jordan and Lex. They both look exhausted, as if they wish they'd never agreed to come, and relieved that they finally get to go. They promise to call soon. And to not tell anyone at school what's happened, to keep this all a secret, although of course that's impossible. I'm pretty sure the hospital's already talked to the school, and people will probably notice when I don't show up in class for forever, since no one will tell me how long I'll be here.

They leave.

I'm taken upstairs, where there are more doctors. They give me a shot of something. I don't know what it is, the shot, but I do know that it's meant to make me more tame and less likely to bite. I don't want it, of course, but it's not a choice.

It's never a choice.

I bare my teeth but hold still. I watch the needle slide into my skin. I feel pain, then nothing. My limbs weaken, but when I'm finally led to my room and given a chance to lie down, my heart beats too quickly and my eyes won't close.

I want ice for all my wounds.

From my spot by the window and through the sinking haze of my mind, I try making sense of my surroundings. There's only one bed, so I guess I won't have a roommate. I don't know why that is. There were other kids out in the hall, I saw them, but I can't speculate if my isolation is a good sign or a bad one. Whatever it is, being here, alone, is in sharp contrast with that first day at boarding school years earlier, when a fourteen-year-old Lex burst into our dorm room. He had streaks of blond in his dark hair and arms full of drum equipment. He ran his mouth from the moment he laid eyes on me, babbling on about his girl-on-girl porn collection, his death-metal tendencies. The force of his exuberance overwhelmed me, especially his insistence on discussing masturbation habits in order to avoid any awkward moments. A good idea in theory, perhaps, but personally, I thought having the conversation was far more awkward than anything else that might happen and told him so.

"I just like to put things out there," he said happily. "I mean, we're roommates. That's almost like being brothers. So no secrets, okay?"

I hesitated. Everything about me was a secret. "Okay."

He grinned. "You can tell me anything."

It's not long before a guy in a hospital staff uniform comes to check on me. He doesn't knock; he just comes right in. He records my vital signs. He leans down to look at me.

"How are you doing?" he asks.

I don't answer. I can't move my mouth. I can't lift my head.

"Are you having a panic attack?"

Am I?

"You're hyperventilating," he explains. "You need to breathe slowly."

I can't do that either.

He flips through my chart. "I can see if you can have something else to help you sleep. Like Xanax or Ativan. Do you want me to do that?"

Still, I can't talk, but he must see something in my eyes. Horror. Despair.

His voice softens. He puts the chart down. "Got it. No Xanax for now. Just try and breathe, okay? I'm going to stay with you."

chapter
thirty-eight

the wolf

I am not new to therapy.

I know the questions they will ask.

I know the answers I can give.

I know the diagnosis I will receive and the medications they will put me on.

None of it will fix me.

The day Keith, Siobhan, and I decided to die did not give me PTSD. Seeing their ruined bodies pulled from the river was consequence, not truth. Reaction, not trauma. That's what everyone forgets.

The pact between us was never the problem.

It was the answer.

"Tell me about your wolf," the doctor says. He sits across from me and presses his fingers together to form a tiny steeple.

"He's stuck," I say.

"Where?"

"Inside of me."

"What does that feel like?"

"What do you mean?"

"What does it feel like to have a wolf stuck inside of you?"

"Oh. It makes me feel broken. Like I'm broken. I mean, I'm sixteen. I'm old enough. I should be changing. That's how nature works."

"What does your wolf look like?"

"How should I know?"

"You've never seen it?"

"No. But I . . ." My mind flicks back to what I saw in the meadow on the way up here. A young wolf that glowed like honey. "I had a vision of what my sister would have looked like. She was beautiful. A brown wolf. Very nimble and graceful. Maybe mine would be similar."

"You think?"

"It makes sense."

"By vision, do you mean you saw something that other people could not see?"

"I suppose," I say.

"Your sister's dead."

"Yes."

"Your brother, too."

"Yes."

"But they had wolves inside of them?"

"Yes. We all did. But they never changed. Keith was fourteen when he died. Siobhan was only seven. She was . . ."

"She was what?"

"Good. She was a good girl."

"How did they die?"

"They jumped off a bridge. A train trestle. Back in Charlottesville."

"I see."

"They didn't want to change," I say.

"And you?"

"I did. I do."

"You wanted to live," he says.

"You say that like it's a good thing. A virtue."

"What is it really?"

I think about this. "Selfish."

"Wanting to live is selfish."

"Yes. Siobhan and Keith, they knew what we were. What the future held for us. And we all made a pact not to become . . . that. To never grow up and hurt anyone. But I wasn't strong enough. I'm weak. And so I lived."

The doctor's lips part, but we both know he doesn't have the right words.

"Your mother," he says finally. "Does she have a wolf inside of her?"

"Oh, she must. She married one. She let us be raised by one."

"I've spoken to her, you know. She tells me she suffers from depression. She has for a long time. She blames herself for what happened."

"She shouldn't. It wasn't her fault."

"Whose fault was it?"

I don't answer.

"Was it Keith's?"

I still don't answer, but I'm not surprised by the question. It's what people usually think. That Keith was sick and persuasive. That Siobhan and I were naïve and corruptible. They're wrong, of course, but that's no one's business but mine.

"Your parents separated soon after," he says.

I stare at my feet. That's when the hive inside of me heats up. It fills my ears with its caustic drone and beads my upper lip with sweat.

"Yes," I manage. "But what happened, that wasn't the only reason they split up."

"What was the other reason?"

"My father got sued by a former student. He lost his job. It humiliated him."

"Where is he now?"

"I don't know. I don't see him. If I did, I'd . . ."

"You'd what?"

Every part of me trembles. I shake my head.

The doctor leans forward. His chair squeaks. "Tell me about your father's wolf."

"I'd like to lie down," I whisper. "I'm tired."

"You haven't been eating."

"They won't let me run. I need to run."

"You have a history of starving yourself," he says gently.

I lift my head. I meet his gaze. "I have a history that I don't like to talk about."

chapter
thirty-nine

relativity

They don't tell me who it is. They just say I have a visitor.

I know it's not anyone from school. They're all in class right now. Third period; I'm missing French. Besides, they'd call ahead first. It can't be my mother, either. It's been only a week since she left, and she's not due back again until November. Her last visit didn't go that well. There's so much that stands between us. I'm too angry. She's too grim. And no, she's not the one I'm mad at, but she's the one that's *here*. We're trying, I guess, and we'll keep trying, but I don't know. Maybe I'll always be that child writhing on the floor, begging to be held.

Maybe she'll always be that mother who can't bear to pick me up.

It's a mystery, then, whoever it is that's come to see me. There aren't a lot of other people who have been in my life. Especially after. That is by design, of course, so I think about before. There's Phoebe. And Lee. Soren Nichols, even. And Anna. There's always Anna. I don't think she'd ever come to see me, though. Not because she doesn't think of me fondly, although that may have changed, but because I remind her of the bad parts of herself. Her guilt. I understand that.

Avoidance is something I will always understand.

I rise from my bed. I run my fingers through my hair and look down at my clothes. I've got jeans on and a striped rugby shirt. My mom brought new clothes for me when she came, and Mr. Byles brought old ones from school when he came, too.

I walk down the hall. I am apprehensive but not afraid. I step into the waiting room and I see her. It's been years, of course, but I recognize her immediately. She's fulfilled the golden promise of her youth. The long red hair. The legs. The fire in her eyes.

"Charlie," I say.

She looks up. She is not happy to see me. But she hugs me. Her breasts press against my chest and it embarrasses me to feel aroused, that queasy stirring of instability. Charlie is a beautiful young woman. Keith would be her age now. She is twenty.

It seems foolish to ask why she came, because the fact of the matter is she did. But I have to know. I take a deep breath.

"We can sit in the garden," I say. She nods. There is an atrium in the center of the hospital, and above us the sky is clear. We sit among lush clusters of ferns and snaking vines. The trickling of water down a copper fountain reminds me to go slowly.

"My mother said you were here," she tells me. "I'm at UVM. Just down the road. Funny, huh?"

Well, no, being in a psychiatric ward, even voluntarily, isn't really funny. But I push my lips into a smile.

"I wouldn't have recognized you," she says. "You're very handsome now. Like all grown up."

"Thank you."

"Your brother was more handsome."

"I know," I say.

She digs around in her purse. It takes a while for her to find what she's looking for. I sit and say nothing, although I feel restless.

"Here!" She shoves something at me. It's a photograph from that summer. Me, ten years old, sitting cross-legged on our grandfather's boat. The blue lake stretches to the horizon beyond. I have a crooked smile and my eyes are squinting. My hair is lighter. Anna's feet are behind me. Ten pink toes, like worms. Or wishes.

I smile again.

"I think you threw up about five minutes after I took this picture," she says.

"Yeah, I did."

"Keith was so mad."

"Yeah."

"You still get sick on boats?"

"I don't go on boats."

She frowns and plays with her hair. "He was really mad at me that day, though. Keith."

"You said that. I remember."

"I've felt guilty about it ever since . . . what happened to him."

"Why? What happened, it had nothing to do with you. Trust me."

Her warm hand squeezes mine. She smells like citrus and sugar. "He told me, Drew. About your dad and the abuse. How he drugged you and did . . . other stuff, those terrible things. Keith told me when we were in New Hampshire. The first night there. It was—it was after you cut yourself at Gram's. You remember that?"

I am numb. I understand her words and I should feel something, but I don't.

She *knew*.

Charlie leans in. "I laughed at him. I said he was making it up for attention."

I hold my breath.

"I know we weren't close, Drew. I don't think you liked me at all. But Keith, he was so *deep*, like profound, you know? I liked it at first, and then it sort of scared me. I thought he wanted something else. But now I think he just really needed someone to tell. A true friend. And I've always wondered if I'd done something, would they still be alive. That's on me, I know that. But if there's anything you need, ever, you let me know. Okay?"

If I nod, will that make her feel better? Is that what she wants? I feel like I should be angry and therefore deny her any satisfaction or sense of redemption. But that requires bitterness, and I'm already too full of bitterness. So I reject this interaction and remain neutral. I reserve the right to think about this all at a later time. Just not right now.

"Tell me about your sisters," I say.

Charlie's lips purse and she sticks her chest out. Maybe she and I aren't so different. We're both reactive. We're both middle children. We're both competitive. Born rivals.

"Phoebe's a senior in high school," she says. "In Lexington. She's like a math genius, though. She's already taking classes at MIT."

"Good for her."

"And Anna is at Oxford, a graduate program. She's studying

public policy. Oh, and she's getting married next summer."
Charlie shifts around in her chair. "She wanted to know how
you were. She asks about you a lot."

I nod. I force nice words out. I do not say what I remember
about Anna. What I know. She killed a man that night. She and
Ricky. They were drunk and they hit a hitchhiker on a moonlit
New Hampshire road after screwing around in the middle of
the woods. They stopped and they touched him and they left him
in the bushes on the side of the road. Then they burned their
clothes and never looked back.

I didn't put the pieces together at first. I was too young. But
when we returned to Massachusetts, I happened to read an
article about the hit-and-run in the *Boston Globe*. And I *knew*.
But I kept my mouth shut. And when it came to my brother and
his pain, I guess, Charlie kept her mouth shut, too.

No, Charlie and I really aren't so different.

I successfully navigate my way through the rest of my cousin's visit. I ask questions about her life. I make eye contact at all
the right times. But in the back of my mind, what I'm really
thinking about is Keith and how his sense of duty seeped into
his bones all those years ago, twisting and reshaping him into
something far different from me. Something nobler, but brittle.

I'll never know what kind of magic my brother believed in.
What I do know is that more than anything, Keith wished for
less suffering in this world. And when he couldn't make that
happen, he lost faith in change.

He lost faith in *everything*.

I let Charlie hug me again when she leaves.

Not because I want to, but because she does.

chapter
forty

bonding

Lex and Jordan visit five times over the next six weeks.

They always come together.

The first time they visit, they let me know it was a black bear that killed that guy in the woods. They both trip over their words, eager to tell me about the hunter who tracked the animal down and shot it. I'm not eager to listen, but I do. The second time they come, they bring food: a plate of oatmeal cookies wrapped in plastic, a six-pack of Coke, and some of those protein bars I like. By the third time, I figure out that they're definitely dating. Or something. It's written in the way they tease and touch—their jokes that flow like ritual, the spark between them vividly alive. I am curious. The attraction part is a given, but maybe opposites really can coexist in peace. I mumble something about hadrons at their next visit.

Lex mishears me. "Hard-ons? Seriously, Winters, I think this place has turned you into a pervert."

I laugh before I can be embarrassed. "Hadrons. That's what it's called when quarks are joined together by force."

"I know what you're talking about," Jordan says. She sits beside me. Her words and movements feel measured. Maybe she's worried what I'll think. Of her. Of them. Of myself. But when Lex runs outside for a smoke, I tell her I think they're good for each other. They deserve to be happy.

She smiles. "You deserve happiness, too."

We sit on my bed and look out at the lake. The trees are all bare. Winter is close.

"You've gained weight," she says. "It looks good."

"It's the medication."

"Or maybe you're hungry."

I think about this. "Maybe."

"Will you come back to school?" she asks.

"Yeah. After the holidays, I think. But I'm going to be a day student. Teddy's family has said I can stay with them. My mom went to college with his father. They've all been, just cool, you know, about this."

"So do you feel better? Has being here helped?"

"Helped what?"

Jordan rolls her shoulders. "I don't know what to call it. You say you're not depressed. You say you're not suicidal or hearing voices. But you agreed to come here."

I look at her. I take her in. That short hair. Those dark, dark eyes.

Yes, it's helped, I want to say, followed by, *But you've helped more.*

It doesn't come out like that, though. My body surprises me. My throat closes up. Tears brim, then spill, wetting my cheeks. A flash flood of misery.

She's alarmed. "Should I get somebody?"

Waves of sadness overwhelm me. With my sorrow comes the simultaneous crash-boom of fear and dread. It's inescapable. I shake my head, but I can't stop crying. Maybe if I knew how, I would hold on to Jordan. I would let her comfort me. Instead I hunch and clench my fists and let this storm of emotion run its course.

I look at her again when I can.

"It's okay," she says.

"I'm sorry."

"Don't be."

"It's not easy to talk about."

"I understand."

"My doctor says that sometimes when things happen to kids, like really little kids and really terrible things, they don't know how to make sense of it all. So they come up with ways of understanding the world that don't look like how other people think things work. Almost like a new language."

"A private language," she says.

Yes.

"He calls it a system of meaning," I explain.

"You're saying something bad happened to you when you were a little kid?"

"I'm saying that my system of meaning about life, about death, everything, is sort of messed up. But . . ."

"But what?"

"But it doesn't mean I'm dangerous. That's what I've learned. That's what's helped me."

Jordan frowns more, and I know I've made her sad. Maybe she's wondering what it is that happened. Maybe she's wondering who it was that hurt me and why my greatest fear is ending up just like him. But then again, maybe she knows.

Because blood is blood, and every family has its own force.

Its own flavor.

Its own charm and strange.

chapter
forty-one

spring

I still don't feel the presence of God.

But from where I sit beneath the dappled shade of an over-grown sugar maple, I watch as Lex and Jordan race along the riverbank, and warmth fills the air. The sun picks up the glints of life in their hair, their eyes, the flush of their skin. Jordan is faster because she is more determined to win. Lex yells as she pulls ahead and he dives for her feet. They tumble into the grass and their laughter rises above the rush of the water and the call of the birds and the buzz of the deerflies. Jordan's up again in an instant, dancing away from Lex. He remains on his back, gasping for air and clutching at his chest in dramatic fashion.

Jordan says something I can't hear, then turns her head to smile at me. She mouths one word. My name.

Andrew.

I smile and wave back.

And it hits me. I have changed.

Not everything's different, of course. My wolf is still here, dormant, yet so very real. But it's no longer a mystery. It's a part of me. A part that will someday find its voice.

I know this now.

My story did not begin on that bridge, on that sun-washed morning when Keith told us about the paradise waiting for us on the other side. The wind blew through our clothes and through our hair, and the three of us stepped onto that railing together. We held hands and we readied our legs. Then the train whistle blew. I looked at Keith and he looked at me. I didn't have to pull my hand back before they jumped.

He let go.

That was their end, but it was not my beginning. My story began earlier, back in Charlottesville, beneath the light of the moon, at the hands of my father. It's the story that was too big for me to tell, the one that grew to fill the depths of my being and the far corners of my mind. It's how I lost my system of meaning.

But I haven't lost everything.

Somewhere, somehow, adrift in the sea and far from the stars, I've found faith.

In myself.

And that makes all the difference.

acknowledgments

I can't begin to show my appreciation for everyone who has helped bring this book to life. You are all the strengths to my frailties.

Many heartfelt thanks to Michael Bourret, for his kindness and guidance, and for seeing the story in my sparseness; to Sara Goodman, for knowing just what needed to be said and for helping me find my way; and to Eileen Rothschild, Kerri Resnick, Jessica Preeg, Matthew Shear, Anne Marie Tallberg, Talia Sherer, and the whole SMP crew, for being so wonderfully talented and supportive.

Thank you also to my dear friends and early readers: Kari Young, Kathy Bradey, Phoebe North, Kristin Halbrook,

Kirsten Hubbard, Kate Hart, Cory Jackson, Jay Lehmann, Jillian Smith, Karen Langford, Jenn Walkup, Deb Driza, Lee Bross, and everyone at YA Highway and Write Night, for all their brilliance and insight. Special thanks to Jackie Kinville, Pat Sussman, Peter Sussman, and Nathan Cheng for their wisdom and willingness to answer my questions, be it night or day.

Last, but never least, thank you, Sidney, Tessa, and Severin, for always being proud of me. You three are the brightest stars in my sky.